Jack Vance

The Pleasant Grove Murders

Jack Vance

The Pleasant Grove Murders

John Holbrook Vance

Spatterlight Press Signature Series, Volume 22

Published by Spatterlight Press

Cover art by Howard Kistler

ISBN 978-1-61947-139-9

Spatterlight Press LLC

Spatterlight
PRESS
340 S. Lemon Ave #1916
Walnut, CA 91789

www.jackvance.com

Jack Vance
The Pleasant Grove Murders

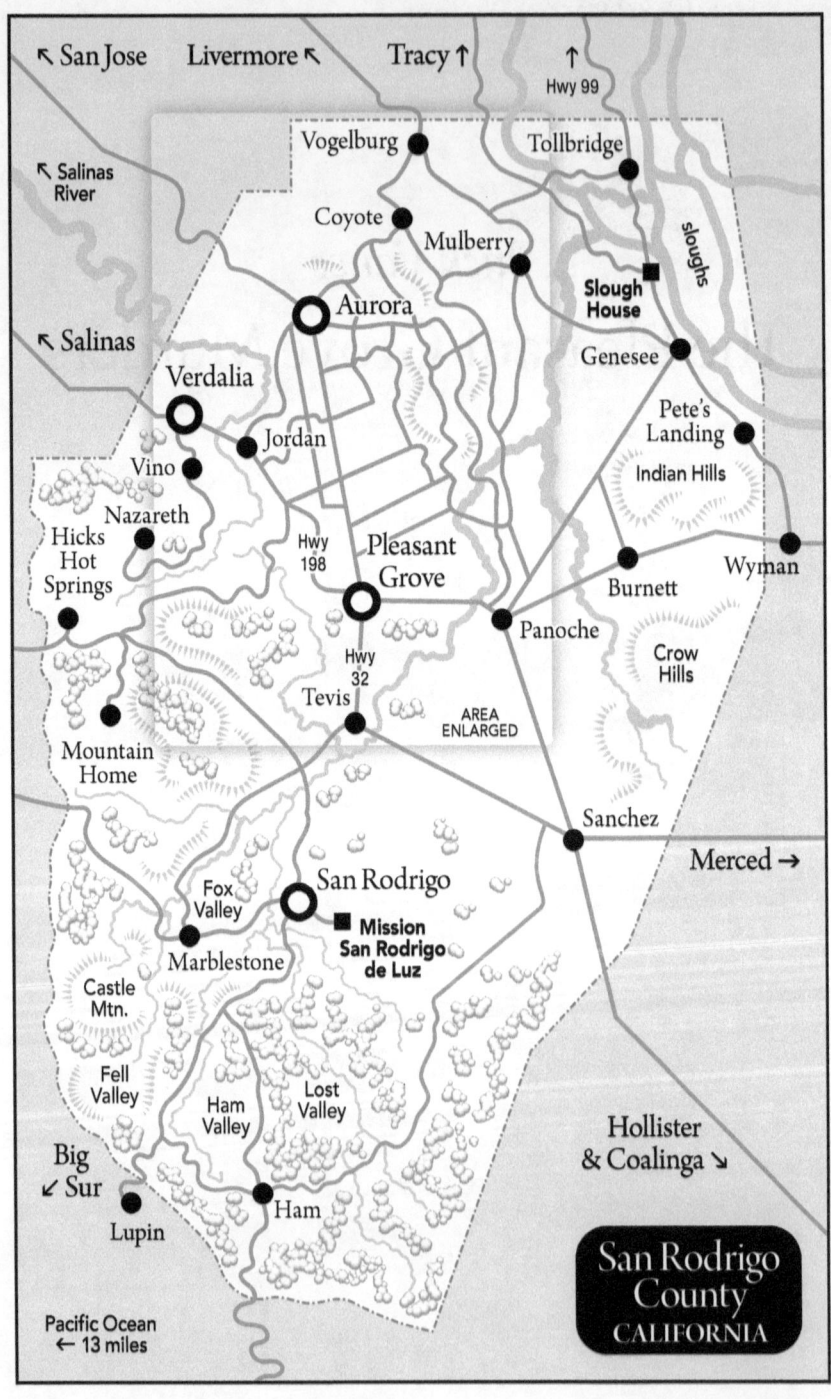

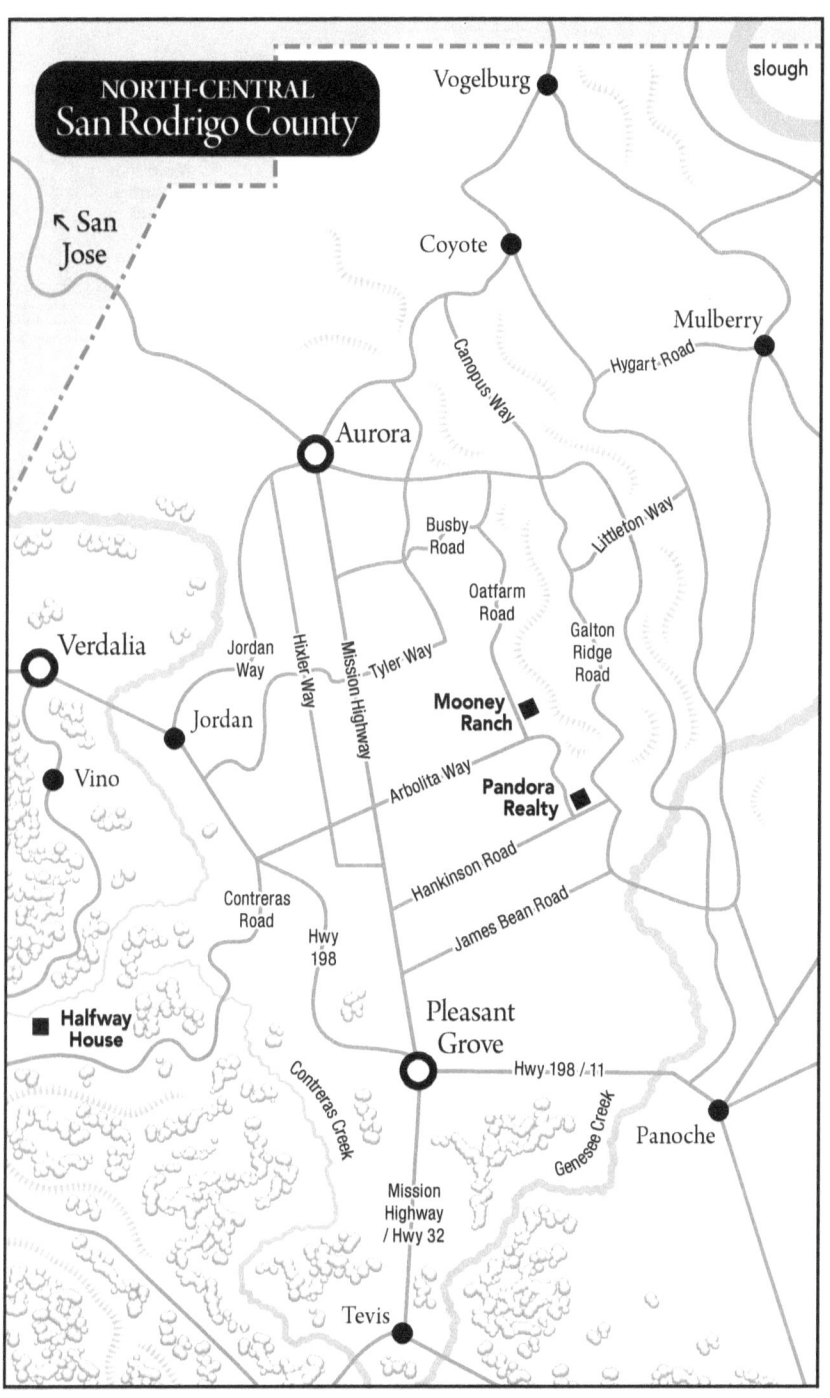

NORTH-CENTRAL
San Rodrigo County

slough

Vogelburg

↖ San
Jose

Coyote

Mulberry

Canopus Way

Hygart-Road

Aurora

Busby
Road

Littleton Way

Oatfarm
Road

Galton
Ridge
Road

Verdalia

Jordan
Way

Hixler Way

Mission Highway

Tyler Way

Mooney
Ranch

Jordan

Vino

Arbolita Way

Pandora
Realty

Hankinson Road

Contreras
Road

James Bean Road

Hwy
198

Pleasant
Grove

Halfway
House

Hwy 198 / 11

Contreras Creek

Panoche

Genesee Creek

Mission
Highway
/ Hwy 32

Tevis

cemetery
wall
MADRONE WAY
golf course
Bazzarini
Mortimer
Hubman
Gentry
Whipple
Wagner
Benjamin
Taylor
Shortridge
Don Luis Montalvo Country Club
McClellan Ave.
Spanish Hill
Montalvo Ave.
Courthouse Ave.
Paicines St.
1st St.
2nd St.
3rd St.
Spanish Hill

Aurora & San Jose
Madrone Way
AREA ENLARGED
Don Luis Montalvo Country Club
McClellan Ave.
Jefferson St.
Roosevelt St.
Paicines St.
Mariposa St.
Spanish Hill
Courthouse Ave.
Hardin St.
Vine St.
Margaret St.
Woolsey St.
Bain home
Peach St.
Carlson St.
Montalvo Avenue
Paicines St.
1st St.
2nd St.
3rd St.
4th St.
5th St.
6th St.
7th St.
Valley Blvd. / Hwy 11
Cherry St.
Plum St.
W. Valley Blvd.
Madera St.
Main St.
W. Madera St.
Courthouse
Annex
Montalvo Square
Garage
Oak St.
Verdalia & Salinas
Panoche & Merced
High School
Wilson Blvd.
W. Main St.
W. Oak St.
Mission Highway / Hwy 32
Hwy 198
Tevis & San Rodrigo
Walnut St.
Poplar Ave.
Fairgrounds
Pleasant Grove

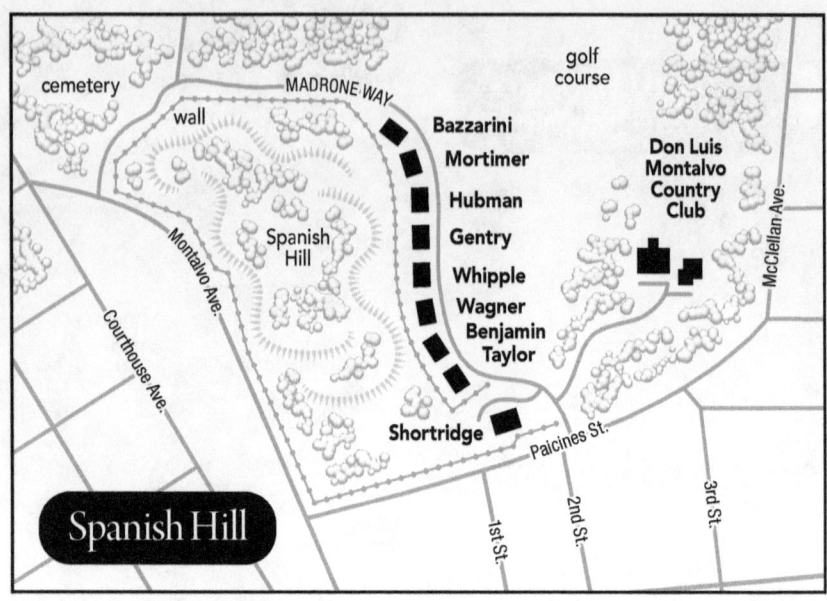

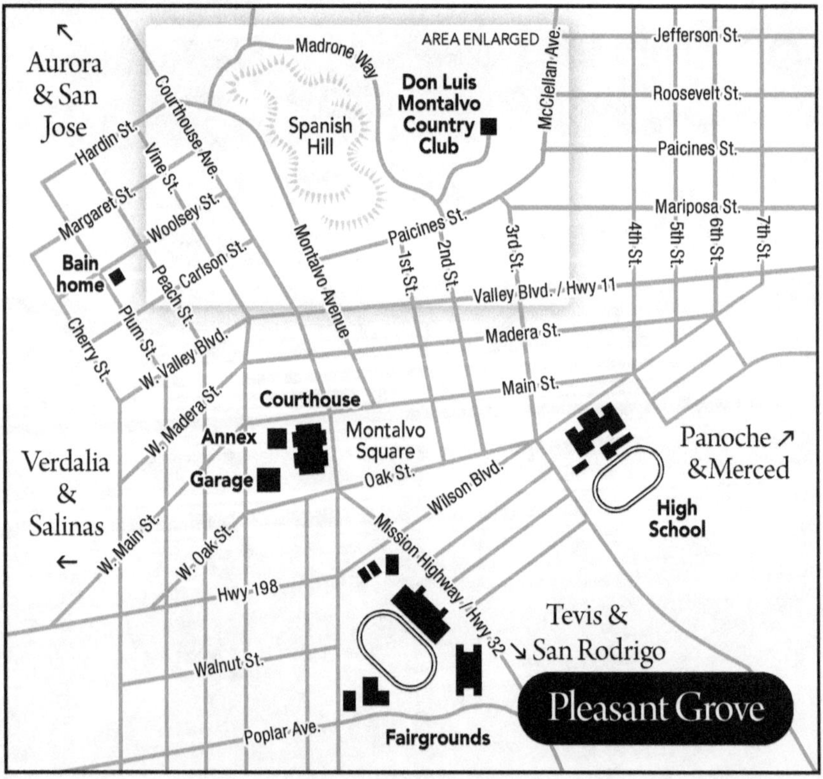

CHAPTER I

1

STARR SHORTRIDGE WAS a notoriously haughty child and had been so for as long as anyone could remember. The explanation was simple: Starr had compared herself to the rank and file of humanity and humanity had come off second best.

At the age of twelve Starr was generally considered insufferable, by all save her father Sam Shortridge, and if Sam Shortridge had his doubts, he needed only to consider his son Marsh, six years older than Starr, a dish-faced youth, careful with his money, meticulous with his clothes, a dutiful participant at Sunday School: altogether, a prig.

The two children were completely different. Marsh used a precocious glibness to disarm his elders. Starr's critics, though willing and articulate, found it difficult to particularize her faults. Obstinacy? This implied a bovine stupidity which never could be imputed to Starr. Possessiveness? Starr distributed her belongings with insulting condescension. Brattiness? When departing company which bored her, Starr made the most polite excuses; if required to remain, she suffered in non-committal silence. Vanity? Starr was a handsome girl, a trifle tall for her age, with long well-shaped legs and arms, patrician features, glossy brown hair, gray-green eyes of startling clarity. She kept herself clean but she was indifferent to clothes and showed small interest in boys. In sheer point of fact Starr's faults were indefinable. Her intelligence was extreme, her imagination extravagant; she found everyone else lackluster and inconsequential, and this was the quality which aroused her critics, who feared that she might be right. The Shortridges, proprietors of Pleasant Grove's largest department store, were the elite of

Pleasant Grove; far easier pointing to family wealth and social position as the source for Starr's arrogance.

Starr's grandfather, who had founded Shortridge's, had also bought Spanish Hill on the northern outskirts of Pleasant Grove. In 1910 he built a grand mansion in the style of a Norman manor house, and to enforce privacy he enclosed the entire property within a seven-foot stone wall. A horticultural enthusiast, he grubbed poison oak and blackberry from Spanish Hill, nurtured the native oaks and madrone, planted cypress, elm, chestnut, ash, walnut, maple, as well as a number of unlikely exotics.

A half century later the plantings were mature, the trees tall, the bowers dank and deep. On a sunny Sunday morning Starr Shortridge took the police dog Henry out for a walk. She climbed the gravel path, back and forth through the pleasant hillside park, under rhododendron, Spanish cork, yew, umbrella pine, Agrigento cypress. The path terminated at a knob of rock surveying all of Pleasant Grove, the surrounding fields and orchards. Directly below was the old house with the mansard roof and double wings. To the west rose the Coast Range; to the east spread the vast expanse of the San Joaquin Valley.

Henry chased a squirrel. Starr called him back and continued north along the ridge. The oaks grew tall, filtering the sunlight through high whispering clots of green. Pleasant Grove became remote: the world consisted wholly of trees, an occasional outcrop of lichen-stained rock; Starr could easily believe herself far away, long ago, in an antique Celtic forest...

She stopped short. On the ground was a litter: scraps of lumber, crumpled paper bags, a saw, an old wood-handled hammer with a broken claw. She looked up the trunk of a sprawling oak to a tree-house of ambitious size, scope and ingenuity.

Starr's eyes sparkled with wrath. Not only was her proprietary sense outraged, not only had there been trespass, but the illusion of sylvan wildness had been destroyed. She marched forward, picked up the old hammer, and climbing to the first landing began to knock away the braces which supported the tree-house.

Instantly a boy about fifteen years old looked out the door. "Hey! What the bloody hell do you think you're doing? Get away from there!"

Starr recognized the boy to be Bill Whipple, of low social status and unsavory reputation, whose father owned a garage and wrecking yard on Courthouse Avenue.

Emerging from the tree-house, Bill stood on the little deck in front. Starr retreated to the ground, and Bill, swinging down to the landing, peered askance at her, legs apart, head cocked forward, eyes sharp and feral. He was a lad of arresting appearance, tall and spare, with a thin harsh face, coarse sandy hair, a big hook of a nose. If he were aware of his low social status or the fact of his trespass, he gave no sign of either: in fact he behaved with insulting assurance, as if Starr were the interloper. He scrutinized her with great intentness: the black ribbon in her hair, her face, her blouse and skirt, bare legs, socks and white shoes. His mouth twitched; jumping to the ground he wrenched the hammer from her grasp. He pretended indignation. "You broke the claw!"

"I did not," said Starr. "It was that way when I picked it up."

"Hell, why worry?" Bill grinned. "Are you worried?"

"No."

"If you're not, I'm not." Bill tossed the hammer aside and came closer. Starr swayed back half a step. She was still too young to derive emotion from anything but horses, dogs and dream-heroes; nevertheless Bill's proximity aroused atavistic tingles along her skin.

Bill seemed to find her presence not unwelcome. He grinned again. "Come on up, I'll show you my house."

Starr gave her head a shake, backed away. Bill hooked his finger in the neck of her blouse. "Just a minute. Do you know what happens when girls come hammering rap-rap where they shouldn't?"

Starr looked over her shoulder. "Henry!" Henry came trotting forward. "Sic 'em." Henry gave a deep snarl and lunged forward. Bill sprang up the ladder, with Henry pursuing as far as the landing.

Starr, smiling coolly, took hold of Henry's collar and pulled him back down to the ground. She called up to Bill. "You'd better leave right now. This is private property. We don't want any junk on it. You or your tree-house. And don't come back."

Bill weighed the situation. Slowly he descended the ladder. Henry tugged against Starr's constraint, growled. Bill's mouth twisted wryly. For two seconds he stood looking at Starr, who gave him back a composed stare. Bill turned away, departed without haste, without shame, managing even something of a swagger.

Starr watched him disappear through the trees. Scowling she turned back the way she had come. Her walk was spoiled, her mood broken. Perhaps never again, she thought, would the illusion return, perhaps never again would the forest seem enchanted. Starr heaved a deep sigh. "I suppose I'm too old for that sort of thing...I'm no longer a child."

Sunday dinner at the Shortridges', served at two o'clock, was a huge old-fashioned meal at which there were usually guests, Sam Shortridge being a gregarious man who enjoyed extending hospitality. Today the guests were the new neighbors who had bought the old Roberts house on Madrone Way: Guy and Grace Benjamin, with their daughter Alice, an extremely pretty girl of Starr's age. Starr, maintaining her usual reserve, watched and listened, and decided that she rather liked Alice, who, in spite of her silky blonde hair, her blue eyes and delightful features, seemed rather shy and not at all 'common', as Starr labeled girls who were too obviously interested in boys or too anxious to make themselves conspicuous. When school restarted in the fall, Starr and Alice would be in the sixth grade together.

During a pause in the conversation Starr mentioned the tree-house. Sam Shortridge frowned, started to speak, but Marsh in a pompous voice exclaimed, "What a lot of nerve! Building such a thing on our property! I think we definitely ought to do something about that!"

"Good idea!" remarked his father. "You can go up this afternoon and knock it down."

Marsh opened his mouth to protest, closed it again. He seemed to have irritated his father, but for the life of him he couldn't understand why.

After dinner Marsh, with Starr and Alice for company, marched up Spanish Hill to demolish the tree-house. With his father not on hand to squelch him, Marsh became more pompous than ever. He declared the tree-house to be an outrage, the more so since the perpetrator had been Bill Whipple, a boy whom he disliked and distrusted. Starr paid no attention and Marsh addressed himself to Alice, who responded with politeness and charm. Starr thought that Alice seemed at once very young for her age and very mature — innocent yet perfectly poised.

And she watched Marsh with sardonic amusement as he sought to impress Alice with the profundity of his experience. It developed that the Benjamins subscribed to the Catholic faith. Marsh, an Episcopalian, analyzed and compared the two creeds, and sought to steer Alice along the path of truth and enlightenment. Alice, with a smiling side-glance toward Starr, shook her head.

They came to the tree-house and Marsh marveled anew at the presumption of Bill Whipple. "Why does he think we've got the place fenced in? If we wanted every Tom, Dick and Harry up here, we'd make the place a public park!"

"It's a nice tree-house," said Alice. "He went to a lot of trouble."

Marsh became exercised; this was the wrong thing to say. Alice did not seem to understand the sanctity of private property and the enormity of Bill Whipple's offense. With ostentatious energy he began to demolish the steps and the landing. Starr spoke from the side in the quietest of voices: "If you knock down the stairs you won't be able to get up to the house."

Marsh pretended not to hear, but presently climbed up to the house proper. He battered, pried, panted, heaved; the tree-house tumbled to the ground, where it lay, a grotesque caricature of its former self. The girls watched uneasily, sensing symbolic portents.

Marsh surveyed the heap of broken lumber. "That's that. I'll send Manuel up tomorrow to burn it, or haul it away…Young Whipple would be wise not to show himself around here again."

Alice listened with drooping mouth. "We live just down below, you know," she said in a tentative voice. "Would you mind if I came up once in a while?"

Marsh indulgently patted Alice's head. "My stars no. Come up as often as you like. Just don't build tree-houses, or leave a lot of trash around."

Catching Starr's eye, Alice almost giggled. Starr smiled her cool smile. In spite of Alice's earnestness and her Catholicism, which Starr lumped together with Marsh's Episcopalianism, she rather liked Alice.

When the three returned to the house Starr studied Alice's parents with a new interest. Guy Benjamin was a civil engineer employed by the State Department of Highways. Grace Benjamin was a humorless woman of meticulous gentility and prim good looks. Starr was reminded of the Puritan women in her American History texts. Guy Benjamin was more like a captain in the Confederate Army: a graceful soft-spoken man with polished bronze hair, a dashing mustache, a tendency toward dry understatement. Grace Benjamin, in contrast, neither understated nor overstated; she simply stated. Occasionally Guy Benjamin's mustache drooped wryly. Alice's Catholicism came from her mother; Guy Benjamin admitted that he never went to church, earning himself a disapproving glance from Grace.

In due course the Benjamins took their leave. Sam Shortridge, returning to the living room, remarked that they seemed pleasant people and an asset to the neighborhood.

"Alice is certainly a beautiful child," remarked Miriam Shortridge. "A regular little Dresden figurine!"

Sam gave an acquiescent grunt. Marsh said brightly, "Yes, she is quite pretty, isn't she?"

Sam Shortridge smiled grimly. "What did you do to the tree-house?"

"I knocked it down from the tree. I thought I'd send Manuel up to burn it."

Sam Shortridge gave the plan short shrift. "He'd set the hill afire. The two of you go up there, bundle up the trash and bring it down-hill."

"Cripes, Dad! There's a ton of stuff up there!"

"Come now. If Bill Whipple carried it up, you and Manuel can carry it down."

"We ought to make Bill Whipple clean the place up," Marsh grumbled. "He made the mess."

"Why create a big scene?" demanded Miriam with a hint of impatience. "It's just a tree-house. The less we have to do with people like the Whipples the better."

Sam Shortridge leaned back in his chair. His own views in regard to social stratification were not quite so clear-cut as those of his wife, and were rather more pragmatic. Still, he considered egalitarianism a debilitating ideal, and so he instructed his children — neither of whom, in their different ways, needed any such instruction.

2

Two doors north of the Benjamins' was the residence of Mr. and Mrs. John Roberts, who long ago had owned the acreage now occupied by the country club. Mr. Roberts died; Mrs. Roberts put the house up for sale and went to San Jose to live with her son, and who should buy the property but Fred and Sheila Whipple, proprietors of Whipple's Garage. Not long after, Fred Whipple took over the Chevrolet dealership and thenceforth went to work in a white shirt and bow tie.

After glacial deliberation the Whipples were acknowledged to be residents of Madrone Way. The Benjamins, on the other hand, were accepted immediately, though they were known to be far from wealthy, and occasionally were patronized: a situation which troubled Guy Benjamin not at all, for he was seldom home. Grace Benjamin bore the subtle condescensions, when they occurred, without change of expression. Alice, as charming as she was beautiful, and vain only to the most inconsequential degree, never even noticed.

CHAPTER II

1

SAN RODRIGO COUNTY, a few hours' drive southeast of San Francisco, had the good fortune to lie aside from the zones of frantic development which were destroying much of the California countryside. The freeways joining San Francisco and Los Angeles ran to east and west; the resorts and scenic areas — Monterey, Carmel, Pebble Beach, Big Sur, San Simeon — lay along the Pacific to the other side of the Coast Range. San Rodrigo County's single tourist attraction was mouldering Mission San Rodrigo de Luz, although the old county courthouse had been cited in Werner Neubarth's book *Toward a New Century* as the nation's most extreme example of that architectural style known as 'fish-market Gothic'.

To the north and east of Pleasant Grove was a tumble of low rolling hills, a spur of the Diablo Range. Among these hills, on a weather-beaten old ranch, Ken Mooney had been born.

Mooneys had lived in San Rodrigo County for as long as anyone could remember. Originally they were important folk: Judge Mooney sat at the first session in the county courthouse; Herman Mooney owned the old Valley Hotel in Aurora, which burnt to the ground in 1882, whereupon he built Halfway House on Contreras Road.

After the first World War the family declined, and presently only a few old-timers remembered the quality of the early Mooneys.

Ken, a big easy-going lad, attended high school at Pleasant Grove, where he distinguished himself principally on the football field. This was the best time of Ken Mooney's life; he was liked by everyone; his amiability disarmed the most surly of individuals, with the exception of his father, who wanted Ken to work harder at home and do less 'fooling around after school'.

Ken's principal weakness was girls. He liked their faces, their voices, the way they walked, the way they sat down, the way they smelled, the way they felt. He liked some girls more than others, but he was not fussy. A girl was a girl, and if Ken couldn't date one, he'd try another, or another, or another, until finally he made a connection, even if she were the sorriest scarecrow around.

During Ken's senior year at Pleasant Grove High, an exquisite blonde girl named Alice Benjamin entered as a freshman. Like every other boy in school, Ken's heart turned over, and all he could think was 'Alice, Alice, Alice'.

To no avail. Alice lived on Madrone Way, across from the country club. Alice's mother was extra-religious, extra-strict, extra-choosy. Ken Mooney, the amiable not-too-particular boy from a hill-country ranch, didn't stand a chance.

In the same class with Alice was Starr Shortridge. Her mother had wanted to send Starr to Miss Hamlin's in San Francisco, but Starr refused point-blank. As proud, aloof, unreasonable, capricious and unresponsive as ever, Starr enrolled at Pleasant Grove High School, where her vagaries exasperated the faculty as much as they did her family. Alice Benjamin thought Starr was wonderful. Alice admired Starr's independence, her coolness, her spirit. Starr liked Alice because Alice liked her. Alice's grades were uniformly good: As and Bs. Starr refused to study and shamelessly took home Cs, Ds and Fs. Sam Shortridge stormed; Miriam Shortridge imposed strictures; Marsh sneered. Censure, persuasion, threats were ineffectual. Even Alice was moved to expostulate.

"Rats," replied Starr. "It's all eyewash. 'Silas Marner' is drivel. 'Hamlet' is obscure. Latin is so dead it smells. What good to me is the binomial theorem? I'm not going to be an engineer."

"What if you want to go to college?"

"I don't want to go to college."

"What *do* you want to do?"

"As soon as I can get away from home, I'm going to Europe and buy a motor-scooter and look for haunted castles in Rumania, and maybe werewolves. Things like that."

"It sounds like fun," said Alice wistfully. "I'd like to go too." She sighed. "My mother would never let me."

Starr gave a disrespectful snort. Her opinion of Grace Benjamin was unflattering. In the first place, Starr considered Mrs. Benjamin a religious fanatic. "When you want to do something," said Starr, "go ahead and do it. If you don't, you have only yourself to blame."

Alice smiled wanly. "I suppose you're right. Still —"

"Still what?"

"I don't like to hurt anyone's feelings."

"I don't either," said Starr, "which is why I don't talk to people very much."

"Starr, you're impossible... But I'd like to go to Europe too. And someday I will! Maybe we could go together!"

"That would be fun," said Starr. "Maybe we can."

Bill Whipple sat down beside them. "What's the big secret?"

Starr made no reply. The silence embarrassed Alice. She said, "We're talking about going to Europe."

"Nice," said Bill. "Where I want to go is Paris. Ooh la la! Also to the Riviera, to hunt the wild bikini."

Alice laughed politely, Starr gave Bill a frowning glance, wondering why she detested him so. He excited repellent little *frissons* along her nervous system. He wasn't bad-looking, or rather, he was ugly in a striking way.

Ken Mooney halted in front of them, hoping against hope to impress Alice. Starr was hardly aware of Ken. She knew his name; she vaguely realized that he played football and was one of Bill Whipple's friends; otherwise Ken Mooney meant nothing to her, one way or the other.

The bell sounded; they went to their classes.

A week or so later, at Alice's insistent urging, Starr attended a Hi-Y picnic at Bellah Creek Camp, in the mountains west of Jordan.

Ken Mooney and Bill Whipple came along too. The trunk of Bill's car was loaded with beer. Mrs. Tremons, the faculty adviser, ordered them to leave, but the two boys lurked on the outskirts of the picnic.

"Look," said Bill, pointing with a half-empty can of beer. "There's Starr. Smart young ————" and he used an unprintable noun.

Ken looked owlishly in the direction indicated. Starr was a girl, hence a girl. Ken therefore was interested.

"You know what let's do?" said Bill, and he put forward a proposal which astounded and shocked Ken. "Hell," said Ken, "I wouldn't do a thing like that. You know it. Starr's a decent kid. I'm ashamed of you."

"She's so damn stuck-up! She's just asking for it. It'd do her good."

"You do it then. Don't get me involved. I don't think she's stuck-up anyway. She's just off in a dream world."

"Don't kid yourself, boy. That girl's stuck-up. I know."

"Okay. So you know. Slash open one of them beers, don't hog it all."

But now Mr. Beasley, the vice-principal, approached and ordered them away from the picnic. Ken apologized for causing a disturbance and Mr. Beasley gave him a friendly whack on the back. "We don't want to alarm the ladies. Now you boys drive carefully. I know you've been drinking, and I don't want you to kill yourselves."

The term ended. Ken and Bill were graduated. Bill's grades were good; he had the knack of study, he was facile with words and numbers, and he was offered a football scholarship to San Jose State which he accepted. Ken went directly into the army, where he served something over two years and received a medical discharge.

Returning to Pleasant Grove, Ken decided that the life of a cattle rancher was not to his taste. The hours were too long, the sun too hot, the hills too lonesome. Also he'd have to work under his father: not so good. Clarence Mooney was a fine man, Ken allowed, but too hard to get along with, and extremely careful with money, to boot.

Ken took a job with the Post Office, where the hours were reasonable, the work easy, the pay on time.

About this time Ken's uncle, Charles Mooney, died. His brother Clarence, Ken's father, as sole heir to the estate, came into possession of Halfway House.

Clarence Mooney called Ken out for a conference. "I got this roadhouse on my hands. You know what it's like; you've been out there."

"Nice old place," said Ken warily. "It sure needs work."

"Here's my proposition. You bring the place up to snuff. Make repairs, fix things up, run the place like it ought to be run. There's a bar, a liquor license, a restaurant — even a hotel, if you want to put that back in operation. Lot of money in a place like that if it's handled right. I'll take half the profits. When I die you'll get the place for your own. What do you say? Won't cost you a cent except what you put into improvements — and that'll come back to you in the long run."

Ken rubbed his chin, wondering where the catch was. His father seldom gave anything away.

"If you don't like the deal," said Clarence Mooney, "I'll put the place on the market. I don't know how much it'll bring, but somebody is sure to buy. There's going to be tourists coming down this way. I say, take them for all they're worth."

Ken decided that his father had no hidden motivation, that the proposition was simply as stated. "Okay. It's a deal. I fix the place up, you get half the net. But one thing we got to agree on: I run the place the way I want to. I don't want to do something and have you come out and tell me I'm all wet. I mean, I just don't want any interference."

Clarence Mooney didn't like the condition, but he agreed. Father and son shook hands; the deal was struck.

When Ken inspected Halfway House, he found more dilapidation than he had bargained for. Everything needed doing at once. Still he was pleased with his acquisition. The place was beautifully situated under a virgin stand of redwood trees; the old porch, the old windows, the old wood exuded old-fashioned good cheer. The bar was crowded with curios and old photographs; there was even a small dance floor. A wonderful place for parties, thought Ken. A wonderful place to bring girls, with the hotel so handy. He arranged with an old man named Wilbur Baker to take care of the bar, which did enough business to pay taxes, electricity, with a few dollars extra for Wilbur Baker.

Every weekend Ken worked on the structure, replacing glass, repairing the porch, waxing the redwood panels in the bar. Presently his enthusiasm began to wane. His work seemed to be lost among all the jobs waiting to be done. His father meanwhile became grouchy and complained that Ken wasn't putting enough time and money into the place. "I'm doing all I can," growled Ken. "I can't do more; I don't make all that much money."

"Borrow! Get the place in tip-top shape! That's the way to make money!"

"Okay. I don't mind. But if I make a loan I want to pay it off first thing, before we calculate profits."

"No sir. The loan gets paid from your half. Why shouldn't it be? The whole place is going to you when I die. Do you begrudge me and your mother and the girls a little comfort?"

Ken shrugged. "Just as you like. I don't want to take anything away from you."

But when Ken applied for a loan, the bank officials insisted that his father, the legal owner of Halfway House, cosign the note, which Clarence Mooney refused to do. Conditions remained as before.

2

Marsh Shortridge's first marriage occurred during his last year at Stanford and lasted a month and a half. The girl's name was Beverley Bancock; she was very tall, thin and active as a nervous whippet, and she played clarinet in the Marching Band. They met on a blind date. Beverley showed Marsh some judo holds and laughingly tussled him down upon a bear-skin rug. Displaying his own skill, Marsh rolled Beverley over and over and over and into the next room. A blow of someone's foot thrust the door shut. Two days later they drove at great speed to Carson City and were married.

Everyone in Pleasant Grove was puzzled by the event, except Starr and perhaps Alice. Not long before, Alice had gone out twice with Marsh, with her mother's benign approval. Marsh became intense on the first date, possessive on the second. The third time he called, Alice stammered lame excuses, which Marsh heard in frozen silence. A month later he married Beverley Bancock, and almost as swiftly was divorced. Alice felt depressed and guilty, as if somehow she had been to blame for the marriage. Starr considered the affair hilarious and reported to Alice that Beverley took her clarinet on the honeymoon and practiced faithfully two hours a day.

For a year after the divorce Marsh avoided Alice. Then little by little he allowed himself to relent: first, cool politeness, then neighborliness; next, camaraderie, then tennis dates; presently, a day at the Monterey Jazz Festival. Finally, when Alice was graduated from Pleasant Grove

High School, Marsh declared himself her escort for the ceremonies. Alice agreed without enthusiasm and Marsh, bending low, kissed her hand. All was forgiven.

Starr was likewise graduated, the faculty being anxious to see the last of her. She made no plans to attend the commencement exercises, and only at the last minute yielded to the expostulations of her father and mother. She submitted to cap and gown, received her diploma with indifference. During the speeches she watched the faces of her classmates and speculated regarding their futures. And her own. Alice in white cap and gown, with her rich blonde hair, soulful eyes, pointed chin and drooping wistful mouth, was enchanting. For some indefinable reason Starr felt sorry for Alice. She seemed so sensitive, so vulnerable; her beauty was sure to make her the focus of other people's emotions. And Starr mused upon Grace Benjamin, sitting watchfully in the third row. Guy Benjamin, at work on a dam in Peru, was not present; according to gossip he had changed to foreign employment in order to avoid the rigors of life at 23 Madrone Way.

The ceremonies came to an end. Starr accepted a few perfunctory congratulations and moved off to await her parents, who were talking to Caspar Hubman, the high school principal, and his wife Laura. The Hubmans lived out toward the end of Madrone Way, and were considered smart and somewhat bohemian. Starr suspected that the topic of conversation was herself. Let them talk.

Starr went out to the front lobby to wait. Here stood Alice surrounded by friends, including Marsh. Starr watched impassively.

A young man in brown slacks, a brown and white hounds-tooth jacket turned his head to look at her: Bill Whipple, a student at San Jose State where he majored in Business Administration. Starr felt the tingling along her nerves. An atavistic response to his masculinity? Simple antagonism? It was neither lust nor liking, Starr was certain on this score.

Bill approached with the long elastic stride which was characteristically his. Meeting Starr's gaze he essayed a polite smile. Starr returned a non-committal nod.

Bill proffered his congratulations.

"Thank you," said Starr.

Bill hesitated, then said, "Are you doing anything after this is all over? I mean, a party or something of the sort?"

"No."

"Good. Let's go someplace and relax. Maybe a Martini or two. Or why not champagne? That's appropriate! Champagne!"

Starr slowly shook her head. "No thanks."

Bill, drawing back the corners of his mouth, studied her with head askew, nose and chin jutting. "I don't think you like me."

"Quite right," said Starr.

"But why?" said Bill, his voice rising a petulant note or two. "Am I offensive? Do I have bad breath? Am I a social leper?"

"I don't like anyone very much."

"Me even less."

Starr shrugged stonily. For all his tension and challenge, Bill bored her. His ideas seemed superficial, his ambitions vapid. Starr wanted something different: a person who was intense and broodingly intelligent, perhaps a trifle impractical, but generous and gay altogether. Then she would have so much to give! It might even be, in fact probably would be, love at first sight. Starr was quite willing to take the chance.

"Starr," said Bill in a tentative voice, "let's get married."

Starr was genuinely startled. "Why would you want to marry me?"

"The usual reasons."

Starr looked off across the lobby. "If I ever marry anyone, it will be for unusual reasons, to an unusual man."

"What's usual about me?" Bill demanded.

"Why go into details?"

"Bah!" muttered Bill. "I'm sorry I brought the subject up. And if I weren't a gentleman —"

Marsh appeared, escorting the radiant Alice Benjamin. Bill's attention was diverted from Starr, as it could hardly fail to be. His lips twitched, his eyes narrowed. Starr smiled in grim derision.

"Hello, Bill," said Marsh in an even voice, expressing the polite recognition due a neighbor. "Starr, are you ready to go?"

"Yes, I'm ready."

Marsh noticed Bill's interest in Alice. Very coolly, with an air of long practice, he steered the girls away.

Bill stood glaring after the three. Essentially Starr's estimate was incorrect: Bill had not been distracted by Alice. He thought of the two girls as beings miles apart, and would have used them, had he been capable, for different gratifications. What he wanted from Alice was simple and straightforward; but Starr! The insolent, captious, mocking Starr! Ah, what he would do to her if he had the chance! He was even willing to marry her. He would break her as a man breaks a horse! She would submit, she would become anxious and wan, she would beseech him for his love. Proud Starr humbled! And Bill, breathing deeply, departed the lobby.

3

The summer passed. Sam Shortridge took his family on a leisurely tour of Canada. Starr would have preferred to travel in Europe, alone by choice, and in fact she broached the subject. Sam and Miriam declared themselves against the project and Starr resigned herself to the placid attractions of Banff, Quebec, the Gaspé Peninsula, Maine, Cape Cod, New York. Here Marsh, becoming restive, departed the group and flew back to California. His pretext was that someone should be at home to keep an eye on the business. Everyone knew that he wanted to keep an eye on Alice.

The Shortridges returned to Pleasant Grove in early October, by way of Florida, New Orleans and the Grand Canyon.

Starr found herself at loose ends. Even if she had wanted to continue her education, her high school record was too bad. She discussed going to San Francisco and finding a job. "What kind of job?" demanded Sam Shortridge scathingly. "You don't have commercial skills. You can't type, or take dictation: you can hardly add. Do you want to work in a cannery? As a waitress?"

"No. But there are other jobs. I could be a receptionist. Or a reporter. Or sell things."

They argued, until finally Sam Shortridge was ready to throw up his hands and allow anything, but now Miriam Shortridge made a tremendous scene, and Sam finally laid down the law. "You're too young to be gadding around by yourself. Hardly out of high school! If you want to work, that's no problem. I'll find something for you at the store. You can take over girls' sportswear. I'll put you in complete charge. That ought to keep you busy."

"No thanks. Really, daddy."

"Well, you're not going off to San Francisco and you're not going to those youth hostels in Europe. I can just imagine what goes on."

Starr raised her eyebrows, grimaced, looked scornfully sidewise at her father. "If I want to get into trouble it's as easy here as any other place."

"Maybe so. At least I won't be aiding and abetting the process. Frankly, I don't know what to do with you."

Starr laughed sadly, but put forward no new proposals. She began to spend a great deal of time at the country club, playing tennis and golf and swimming. Occasionally she went out on a date and Sam and Miriam held their breath, hoping she'd fall in love with some decent young fellow and marry. They weren't in any hurry to have her leave home, but matrimony at least was definite. Once Starr was married they could relax. But Starr never went out with the same man twice.

Christmas approached. Guy Benjamin returned from Peru; Alice came home from Mills College, with the doleful news that she was not doing well and very likely would flunk out. Marsh went to great lengths to console her, and one glad night brought home the news that Alice had agreed to marry him. Sam and Miriam were delighted. They approved of Alice, even though they found her parents a trifle difficult. Starr felt sorry for Alice, who, truth to tell, did not seem ecstatically happy over her engagement. "Well, what would you expect?" sniffed Sally Wagner, Madrone Way's most voluble gossip. "They've known each other years and years and it can't be very exciting. Poor little Alice … Still she could do worse. As Mrs. Malaprop said: 'Love and aversion both wear off in marriage, so one might as well start with a little aversion'." And Mrs. Wagner gave one of her great hoarse laughs.

In late February Guy Benjamin was sent to India to supervise the construction of a dam on the Chabna River. In April Alice flew off to Europe to spend the spring and summer with family friends, which induced Starr to reproach her father: "If Alice can go to Europe by herself, why can't I?"

"First of all," said Sam heavily, "she's going to get married, you're not. Secondly, she's not my daughter. Frankly I'm surprised Mrs. Benjamin allowed her that much leeway. Thirdly, you and Alice are two different breeds of cat. Alice does what she's told. You're just the opposite, as obstinate and perverse as a girl can be."

"Father, dear dear father! I'm nineteen years old."

"I know that. In two years you'll be twenty-one. What you do with yourself then is your own business. In the meantime, you're still my little girl."

"But why can't I go to Paris with Alice?"

"Because she's with people who invited her. They didn't invite you."

"I see."

4

Grace Benjamin and Sally Wagner were not on speaking terms, although they had lived next door to each other for many years. The incident giving rise to the coolness was trivial, but given Sally Wagner's brash volubility and Grace Benjamin's icy reserve, unpleasantness became inevitable. The affair, while not immediately antecedent to Sally Wagner's death, constituted a definite link in the chain of events. Had Sally Wagner controlled her tongue — thus remaining on speaking terms with her neighbor — her skull might never have been battered and broken.

Sally Wagner and Grace Benjamin both normally traded at Levison's Pharmacy on Courthouse Avenue. But one morning in early March, not long after the departure of Guy Benjamin for India, Sally Wagner chanced to visit Aurora, twenty miles to the north of Pleasant Grove, and there, in the Payless Drug Store, she discovered Mrs. Benjamin purchasing several bottles of drugs, in a manner unmistakably furtive. Even before Sally Wagner greeted Mrs. Benjamin she peered at the brown plastic bottles, which were labeled *Stuart's Pre-Natal Capsules*. Grace Benjamin, becoming aware of Sally Wagner, made a quick motion as if to hide the bottles; she apparently had been trying to decide whether to buy one, two or three of the hundred-capsule bottles. Sally Wagner, who considered Grace Benjamin something of a stick, could not resist a mock-friendly jibe. She called out in her hoarse throaty voice: "Grace Benjamin! Don't tell me you're expecting again! And at your age!"

Pink rose into Grace Benjamin's cheeks. She was at this time a tall thin-featured woman of forty, notorious even at church for her uncompromising devoutness. Sally Wagner's vulgar bray had attracted amused glances from people standing nearby. Words failed Grace Benjamin. She opened her mouth to speak: once, twice, three times; then, reacting much more vehemently than the situation would seem to warrant, she blurted: "If it's any of your business, yes." And she turned her back.

"Well, indeed!" snorted Sally Wagner, and swept away in a fury of her own. When she later reported the episode to her friends she contrived to make Mrs. Benjamin and her pregnancy as ridiculous as possible, a situation which inevitably came to Mrs. Benjamin's attention.

In such a fashion arose the rift between the two neighbors, and — as an eventual consequence — Sally Wagner came to an unpleasant end.

But first there were other killings.

About ten o'clock on the morning of Tuesday, June 18, Ken Mooney turned his mail van into Madrone Way. Soon after, someone struck him dead with a hammer.

What happened next was a source of enormous puzzlement. Ken Mooney, van and undelivered mail disappeared until the following morning, when all were found at the blind end of Madrone Way.

The mail apparently had not been tampered with; the various bundles, sorted and tied with coarse twine, were undisturbed; all the undelivered registered mail was on hand.

The postal authorities, finding no violation of postal laws, relinquished the case to Sheriff Joe Bain.

CHAPTER III

1

ON THE MORNING OF WEDNESDAY, June 19, Joe arrived at headquarters, made a brief inspection of the jail, had a word with Ace Wardell, the despatcher and desk sergeant, then went into his office and looked over the mail. There were official notifications and circulars, advertisements, letters of protest or accusation, requests for assistance, protection, advice. Mrs. Wilson, of Hygart Road near Mulberry, complained of the unseen agency which pelted her with clods when she worked in her garden. Bill C. Mazaretto of Tevis reported a stolen calf. Tony Silveira on Blue Hill Road outside of Verdalia described a burglarized tool shed, and included a sketch of the broken hinges by which he hoped to facilitate the investigation. Burt Rank, director of the Mosquito Abatement Program, had dropped by a memorandum concerning a woman named 'Luna', which read:

> This woman is a nut. So far so good, but on the side
> she is breeding mosquitoes. Not on purpose. I hope
> she never tries it on purpose. She is conducting
> experiments in interplanetary communication using
> large trays of water, to concentrate the thought-rays.
> She is not bothered by the mosquitoes, who only
> attack smelly sons of bitches like myself. Luna thinks
> I'm a civilian and a clod and won't listen when I order
> her to stop breeding mosquitoes. Please go by and
> drain her thought-ray tanks. She lives behind the
> Pandora Realty office on Hankinson Road.

Joe was lean, something over average height, with neatly brushed black hair, a darkish olive complexion, an expression sometimes wry, sometimes rueful. Separating the letters, he took some in to Ace Wardell, who would notify deputies on patrol. Then, with a sigh and a groan, he settled himself to the others. During the tenure of his predecessor, Sheriff Ernest Cucchinello, a certain Mrs. Rostvolt had handled matters of this nature with silken ease. The new matron, Miss Irene Curdy, formerly employed at Tehachapi State Prison for Women, tended to see things in terms of black and white. Mrs. Rostvolt had been deft and diplomatic; Miss Curdy told people the way things were, with Joe shuddering for votes going down the drain. It looked as if Miss Curdy, so lately hired, might have to be replaced, and soon. But with whom? And how to inform Miss Curdy that her services were no longer required? Joe's mouth twitched…The telephone rang. Joe picked up the receiver to hear the voice of Frank Hardinger, Chief of the Pleasant Grove Police Department. "Sheriff, there's been a killing. Young mail carrier named Ken Mooney. Guess it's your baby."

Joe hitched forward in his seat. "What happened?"

"Seems like he got his head beat in."

"Any line on who did it?"

"I know no more than you. The body is in a post office truck, far end of Madrone Way."

Joe telephoned the coroner, summoned Rex Kelly, one of his new deputies, and departed for the scene of the crime.

2

Joe drove up Courthouse Avenue, through the old Northside district, into Madrone Way between a pair of ornate granite pedestals. Madrone Way made an S-curve, then swept north past a line of fashionable residences, each set back from the road among trees and gardens. Here lived the aristocracy of Pleasant Grove, with the Shortridges, Mortimers and Gentrys at the top, and the Whipples quite definitely at the bottom.

At the far end of Madrone Way, opposite the home of Mrs. Mary Bazzarini, stood the mail van. The body had been discovered by a Miss Locke, day nurse to Mrs. Bazzarini. Arriving at work, she had glanced into the apparently unattended van and discovered the corpse of Ken Mooney, surrounded by bundles of mail spilled from a canvas basket.

The coroner, Dr. William Hesketh, tentatively set the time of death as twenty-four hours earlier, in the neighborhood of ten or eleven o'clock. Ken Mooney had been struck viciously from behind, upon the right side of his skull. At least three blows had been dealt, immediately above the ear and up toward the scalp. There had been little bleeding; Ken Mooney's blue-gray uniform was quite unsoiled. With grotesque fastidiousness the current copy of *Life*, with the address sticker torn away, had been tucked under Ken's battered head. Two postal inspectors from San Jose conferred in hushed voices with Henry Deardorf, the postmaster, who carried his book of registration records, until Ken's body had been transferred into the county ambulance. Then they removed the mail to the sidewalk and checked it over, bundle by bundle.

Deputy Rex Kelly worked around and within the van with his insufflator, blowing fingerprint powder here and there. Hundreds of smudges and smears appeared, as well as a few prints, all of which subsequently proved to be those of Ken Mooney.

Joe's first official act had been to feel the van's radiator and engine block. They were cold. The van had been in place for several hours, perhaps most of the night. He inspected the tires, the exterior and interior, finding nothing which impressed him as significant — except the copy of *Life* under Ken's head. Where the address label had been torn away the page was strained and crumpled. In the undelivered mail were other copies of *Life*.

Joe went to interrogate Miss Locke, who stood watching proceedings from Mrs. Bazzarini's front window. She told him only what she had told Captain Hardinger: that coming to work she had glanced into the van, and after noting the body had gone directly into Mrs. Bazzarini's house and called the police.

Joe next put inquiries to Mrs. Bazzarini, the widow of Salvador Bazzarini, who had founded the Monteverde Wineries in the foothills west of Pleasant Grove. Mrs. Bazzarini was about seventy-five years old, with a waxen skin, fluffy white hair, pudgy cheeks. She seemed extremely upset by the circumstances, and her eyes were rimmed with pink as if she had been weeping. "Such a terrible thing! A terrible thing!" she told Joe.

"It certainly is," said Joe. "Did you notice when the van arrived out in front?"

"No indeed. I was sound asleep. I had a very good night. It could have been any time. He was such a nice boy, so considerate! Who would do a thing like that?"

"I'll do my best to find out," said Joe. "You knew Ken Mooney?"

"Yes; he often came in to talk with me."

"Did he ever mention anything which might have a bearing on his death?"

"No, nothing. It's a terrible, terrible business."

Joe returned outside, to consider the situation while Rex Kelly and the postal detectives completed their work. At least two circumstances seemed worthy of note: the *Life* magazine under Ken's head and the fact that the body had not been discovered until almost a full day after the murder.

Every departure from the normal assists the solution of a crime: so Joe had learned at the Chapman Institute of Criminology in North Hollywood. In this case, he thought, the murder of Ken Mooney looked like a cinch. He went to talk to Postmaster Henry Deardorf, a slope-shouldered man with a tight little potbelly, round brown eyes rendered even more round and brown by his glasses. Henry Deardorf considered the murder an outrage committed not only upon Ken Mooney and the United States Post Office, but also upon himself: "— thirty-one years I've worked in the post office, every department, summer and winter; I've seen every manner of thing, but nothing like this." And he glanced angrily toward the van.

"What do you think happened?" Joe asked.

"I don't know. It's just all this crime and juvenile delinquency."

"You had trouble with Ken?"

"I wouldn't say that. No, nothing like trouble."

"What kind of a fellow was he?"

Deardorf blinked, confused by the need to think. "Well, it's hard to say. I considered him just a little lax, but there's never been complaints about his work. He comes from a good family, one of the few old families left around these parts. There's been Mooneys in San Rodrigo County since I don't know how long."

"Ken lived at home?"

"Yep. Out at the old Mooney ranch."

"Let's see, I ought to know where that is." Joe reflected a moment. "Out Oatfarm Road somewhere, isn't it? Right down in front of a big round hill?"

"That's the place. You go out Hankinson Road until you come to the Pandora Realty, then turn left and go on another two or three miles. I don't imagine Ken spent much time home. Clarence Mooney is a close-handed man, always was."

"Something puzzles me," said Joe. "Ken was killed yesterday morning with only half his route delivered. What happened when he didn't return to the post office? Or maybe you didn't notice?"

Deardorf gave Joe an angry look. "Certainly I noticed. I'm postmaster — it's my job to notice things."

"What time did you notice?"

"Oh, long about three, I guess. Ken should have been in by two."

"Nobody called in wanting their mail?"

"Everybody just decided it was a late delivery, or figured there wasn't mail that day. At four I went out to look for him, and when I couldn't find the van I called back into the office. The girl didn't hear me straight —" Deardorf shook his head in contempt for the incompetence of the clerk "— anyway she gave me to understand that Ken had come back in. I was calling from home, and I just put the matter out of my mind. This morning I learned the right of it. I called his home and they hadn't seen Ken, so I called Chief Hardinger and then the district office in San Jose. Just about that time the lady found the body."

A mixup, plain and simple. And Deardorf explained what he had asked the clerk and what she thought he had asked and how she had responded, and how he had misinterpreted her response. "Can't trust anybody even to talk straight any more!"

"I guess that's right," said Joe. "Well, what about Ken? Did you know any of his friends, anything like that?"

"No sir, I did not. What he did in his spare time was his own business, so long as it wasn't to the detriment of the United States Post

Office. He liked girls pretty well; in fact I've had words with him about what I call over-familiarity. He was just too friendly with ladies. It won't do for a postal official, any more than a police officer, to get on personal terms with the public: not while that man is wearing a uniform. That's an iron-clad rule I laid down, and I've enforced it too, and there's never been any impropriety or misconduct or anything of the sort, as you hear about at some of the stations."

"Hmm," said Joe. "You mean Ken got a little too friendly with women along the route?"

Deardorf turned Joe a look of angry reproach. "Do you think I'd stand for anything like that? No sir! Mooney and all the rest know it."

The postal detectives approached, a pair of mild-mannered men, almost excessively polite. They announced themselves satisfied that no crime against the United States Post Office had occurred. All the registered mail was accounted for; the mail had been delivered the length of Madrone Way as far as the Bazzarini house; the mail bundled for delivery farther along the route was undisturbed. Nodding politely to Joe and Postmaster Deardorf, they went to their car, where one began to dictate a report into a tape recorder, while the other gravely began to eat a tomato and lettuce sandwich.

The body had been conveyed to the morgue; Rex Kelly had finished his search for fingerprints and was collecting material from the floor of the van with a portable vacuum cleaner. The onlookers, a hundred feet away, craned their necks, awed by this demonstration of real-life criminology, even though it failed to match up to TV. It wasn't nearly so interesting. It moved more slowly. There was no action to speak of. The sheriff seemed indecisive and perplexed, as if he did not know what to do first. Joe, noting the critical gazes, took Deardorf around to the other side of the van. "Just what in general was Ken's routine?"

"Same as everybody else's," snapped Deardorf, who by this time was sick of the whole business. "The morning mail is sorted. All hands turn to; we get it routed out; then the carriers pack up and take off."

"Each route is pretty well established then?"

"Down to the last iota. We got to be efficient or we wouldn't get the mail out."

"After Mooney finished Madrone Way, where would he head for?"

"He'd deliver the country club, then the south side of Paicines as far as McClellan, then out McClellan to work what we call Northeast One District."

"But he never got even as far as the country club."

"That is correct. He delivered that house there, the Mortimer house." Deardorf pointed. "That was the last delivery. He never even delivered to Mrs. Bazzarini. Her mail is still in the truck."

"Strange," muttered Joe. "If he delivered as far as the Mortimers' why not make one last stop?"

"It's beyond me," said Deardorf. "Are you finished with the van?"

"I guess we've got everything…Rex, can you think of anything else?"

"Just that *Life*. I'd like to know who it was being delivered to."

Joe nodded. "I've been thinking along the same lines. But I guess we won't hold up the mail on that account. She's all yours, Mr. Deardorf."

The postmaster marched to the van, jumped in, started it with a fastidious twitch of the wrist, and departed north along Madrone Way. Joe turned to Police Chief Hardinger. "You notified Ken's parents?"

"I telephoned out as soon as we heard the news. Just as soon take a beating."

Joe gave a dour grunt. "Let's go over these people house by house, and you tell me what you know about them."

Hardinger rubbed his chin. "I can't see anybody out along here bashing Ken Mooney. These are the best people in town! They don't even like getting a traffic ticket!"

"Offhand," said Joe, "it looks like somebody from the Mortimer house or Mrs. Bazzarini; that's where the delivery stopped."

Chief Hardinger looked off across the golf course. "I hate to tell the sheriff he don't know his business — but Mary Bazzarini is in a wheel chair and Wilfred Mortimer is in Honolulu with his whole family. The house is empty."

"Well then, how about this? Somebody approaches Ken just as he finishes shoving mail in the Mortimer box. He induces Ken to drive the van off somewhere, hits Ken over the head, and hides the van until night, when he brings the van back out here, to the end of Madrone Way."

Chief Hardinger shook his head dubiously. "I suppose anything is possible."

Joe turned to Rex Kelly. "Rex, you go from house to house. Find out who saw what. Ask where people were yesterday morning. Maybe some of them talked to Ken. Maybe they noticed someone riding in the van. Pick up whatever you can get. I'm going out to talk to the Mooneys."

CHAPTER IV

1

JOE DROVE HOME for lunch to the little frame house on Plum Street where he chose to live in spite of the hints of his mother, Marian Bain, and the open disgust of his daughter Miranda, who was now 16 and just through her junior year in high school. Both mother and daughter were proud of Joe, but felt that he didn't take himself seriously. Both thought that the circumstances of his position demanded a more stylish address. To date Joe had resisted their arguments, but the pressure mounted continually. At lunchtime Miranda complained of the two pepper trees which stood in the front yard. "They're so messy, and just far enough apart that I can't tie up a hammock."

"I'll say this," remarked Marian Bain, "nothing will grow beneath them. There's too much oil in the leaves, or maybe it's the pepper. Do you remember what happened to the zinnias last year?"

"Pretty sad," said Joe. "Pass me some salad."

"When we move," Miranda remarked, "I think we should look for a house without pepper trees."

"Who said anything about moving?" demanded Joe. "The roof is tight and the neighbors don't keep dogs: this is my idea of a good house."

"It's shabby," declared Miranda. "It's old and decrepit. You walk across the floor and the windows rattle. You can hear the toilet flush all the way down to the corner."

"Come now," said Joe. "You're exaggerating. Think for a change! This place costs seventy-five dollars a month. It's comfortable, cool, quiet. There's no taxes to pay, no lawn to worry about, there's peach and plum trees in the back. We'd be fools to move!"

"But Daddy, you're *Sheriff*! Aren't you aware of that? You've got a front to keep up! Look where Sheriff Cucchinello lived, on McClellan Avenue!"

"He also had a cooler nerve and a steadier hand than I have. Girls, let's be sensible. We could buy a fancy house, a Lincoln Continental, a big swimming pool with payments to match. Next election I get ousted from the public trough, then what? My only skills are lettuce-picking and poker-playing, and neither pays too well."

"You're just joking, Daddy. You know people are going to vote for you."

"If I behave myself. The old days they called it 'reputation', now it's 'public image'. Suppose I suddenly come forth in a big white Stetson, a new convertible, two or three blondes wearing black underwear. Do you know what people are going to say? 'Aha, that grafting Sheriff Bain!'"

"I think you should do what's right and not worry what people think," said Marian Bain.

"All well and good, except then you get into different problems. Take Howard Griselda and the *Messenger* for instance. Suppose a couple young thugs hold up a service station and Howard Griselda writes about it. If I shoot them, it's brutality. If they shoot me, it's incompetence. If they're young, I allowed juvenile delinquency to flourish. If they're old lags, why didn't I keep my eye on them?"

"Heavens!" said Marian Bain. "Other people have the same troubles. Nobody else gets so upset."

"I'm the nervous type."

"The fact remains that you're making more money now and Miranda should have a nice home where she could bring her beaus."

"This *is* a nice home. Do we need marble statues in the front yard? You make out like it's a shanty."

"Well, you know how girls are. They like to show off just a little."

"She brought her friends here before; did they suddenly get snooty?"

"Of course not. It's just that —"

"The smart thing is to set tight and put our money in the bank. Then one of these days we'll buy some land and build a *real* house. Meanwhile, fix this place up a little. Paint the floor. Plant some more zinnias and some more pepper trees. Crochet some of those 'Home Sweet Home' things for the walls."

Marian Bain sighed and shook her head; Miranda groaned in despair, and stormed off into the living room. Joe grinned wryly. Miranda looked something like her mother, who, eloping fifteen years previously with a cowboy guitar player, had never been heard from again. Miranda was just as pretty, just as vivacious and with a far better disposition. Probably inherited from her grandmother, thought Joe — certainly not from himself. He finished off a piece of cocoanut cream pie and a can of beer, which did not go especially well together. "There's been a killing," he told his mother. "Happened yesterday, young mail carrier. Now I have to go out and talk to his folks."

"*Tcht tcht tcht.* Isn't that awful! Who would do such a thing?"

"I'll find out. I haven't missed yet."

"Who was the boy?"

"Young fellow from up north a ways: Ken Mooney."

"I don't think I know the family."

"They've been around a long time, from what I hear. Well, I've got to go talk to them."

2

There were two routes to the Mooney ranch: north out of Pleasant Grove by the state highway to Hankinson Road, east to Oatfarm Road, north once more to the Mooney Ranch; or east out Valley Boulevard to Galton Ridge Road, north to Hankinson, with a dogleg back to Oatfarm Road.

From Joe's house on Plum Street the route by Courthouse Avenue north was more convenient. The fringes of Pleasant Grove extended a mile or so, with Spanish Hill bulking to the right hand. There were small dusty houses, shaded under dusty black-green eucalyptus, or not shaded at all; business enterprises: service stations; wrecking yards; a hay, feed and fertilizer barn; a plumbing supply house; restaurants with redwood and field-stone fronts; a Big Orange; a Frosty Freeze; a Giant Dog. After a final Bluebell Service Station, a last 19¢ Chuckburger, the country began: orchards — peach, apricot, almond; small dairy farms;

vineyards; truck-gardens; fields of alfalfa; occasionally a stretch of derelict land with a ramshackle barn, a sagging old house. To the left loomed the Coast Range; to the right rolled a complicated system of sunburnt hills, the southernmost thrust of the Diablo Range.

Joe turned east on Hankinson Road, toward the hills. The farms and orchards became smaller, the vineyards somewhat less green. He crossed an enormous irrigation aqueduct, passed a Pacific Gas and Electric sub-station, the untended transformers humming and buzzing. A highway marker warned 'Crossroads Ahead' and Joe saw the sign PANDORA REALTY. Joe muttered, "Pandora Realty?"... Something about Pandora Realty, something in another connection... Joe turned north on Oatfarm Road.

The orchards were no more; the alfalfa was coarse and thin. To the right rose the hills, round tawny shapes merging, swelling, melting into one another, duplicating all the contours of a woman's body. Occasionally, beside a tin mailbox, a dirt road wound away into a valley; occasionally a copse of eucalyptus or oak, a windmill, a weathered gray barn gave witness to some human presence.

The Mooneys lived two hundred yards back from the road in a two-story white clapboard house. In front were a parched lawn and two dwarf lemon trees; in back were a chicken-house, two sheds, a tank and a windmill. Off to the side, half-submerged in weeds and thistles, was the carcass of what might have been a black 1926 Dodge sedan. Joe drove into the yard, halted behind the Mooneys' present car, a tan Chevrolet, about five years old. For a moment or two Joe sat in the car, aware of the leaden woe which seeped from the old house. He looked around for a dog, got out of the car, went up to the door, which opened as he approached. A tall, thin man looked out. He had a bald freckled scalp, a fringe of sandy-gray hair, a bulging forehead, a long nose, a long chin stubbled with gray whiskers. He wore dark brown corduroy trousers, with suspenders across a faded blue shirt.

"You're Mr. Clarence Mooney?" Joe asked.

"That's right."

"I'm Sheriff Joe Bain. I want to talk to you about Ken."

Clarence Mooney gave a curt nod. "Come in."

Joe entered the dim living room.

A small round woman with a mouse-colored tumble of hair sat huddled in an arm-chair. This, thought Joe, would be Ken's mother, bewildered and dazed by the terrible fate which had befallen her son. Two teen-age girls, all arms and legs, sat stiff and still on an old purple-red sofa. The room was sparsely furnished: a round oak dining table, a book-case with twenty or thirty books and at the very center of the far wall, a grand new color TV-stereo combination — an item so lavish as to be incongruous. Joe introduced himself once again. "I'm sorry to bother you at a time like this; I know how you must feel. But I want to catch the person responsible, and I need your help."

Mrs. Mooney lowered her head and began to sob, in shoulder-wrenching moans; the girls sat as if hypnotized. Clarence Mooney walked slowly across the room to the dining room table, pulled out a chair for Joe, then went to stand by the fireplace. "It's something I can't understand. I just plain can't understand it. Nobody hated Ken. Everybody liked the boy."

"Somebody wanted him dead," said Joe. "Bad enough to kill him. Who could it be?"

Clarence Mooney gave his head a shake. "I just don't know."

Mrs. Mooney spoke in a gasping hurried voice: "Whatever the reason, it wasn't against Ken! It must have been something to do with the mail!"

Clarence Mooney reached into a paper sack of tobacco, extracted a small pinch, rolled it between his fingers. "Was anything missing? Money? Packages?"

Joe shook his head. "The mail is all safe. I'm just wondering if Ken had a falling out with one of his friends."

Clarence Mooney tucked the wad of tobacco delicately into his mouth. "He never mentioned it here."

"Ken got along with everybody," declared Mrs. Mooney, in a somewhat calmer voice.

"What did he do with his salary?"

Clarence Mooney looked at Joe wonderingly. " 'Do with his salary'? Same as anybody else. Spent what he needed, put the rest away."

Joe nodded sagely. "Did he ever seem to come into large sums of money, from time to time?"

Clarence Mooney's light brown eyes became hooded. "What do you mean by that?"

Joe gave a non-committal shrug. "Money sometimes is at the bottom of these things."

"I don't know what you have in mind," said Clarence Mooney, "but if you suspect Ken of dishonesty, forget it. He wouldn't steal if he was starving."

"I'm sure that's the case, Mr. Mooney. But we have to check every angle. You didn't notice him, well, spending a trifle too freely, say?"

Clarence Mooney's lips compressed into a small tight smile. "No, sir. I certainly did not."

"Did he ever talk about the people on Madrone Way?"

"Not too much. He knew Bill Whipple from high school. When he was a senior he used to spark around a girl — I can't remember her name, but she lives on Madrone Way."

"Alice Benjamin," said the older of the girls.

Her father turned the girl a quick bright glance. She pulled her head down, drew her shoulders together.

Joe pretended not to notice. "Nothing serious, I suppose?"

"My stars no. The Benjamins, they're up in the social whirl. We're just farming people. Been around here many years though. They named Oatfarm Road for the time my grandfather put our north square in oats."

The older girl, unhunching her shoulders, raising her head, spoke in a quick rush of words: "Ken and Bill Whipple were going into the trucking business, if Ken could sell Halfway House."

Clarence Mooney looked fixedly at a point on the opposite wall three feet above the TV-stereophonic combination. He spoke in a measured voice. "That's nonsense. Halfway House wasn't Ken's to sell. I turned it over to him but I held on to the deed."

"What about this trucking business; was there anything to it?"

Clarence Mooney shrugged. "Just talk. Ken didn't have financing. He wasn't cut out to be a businessman anyway. He didn't have that dog-eat-dog urge."

"You say you let him have Halfway House: you mean that old place out Contreras Road?"

"That's right. My great-granddaddy built that place, nearly a hundred years ago. It was real stylish in those days. Now—" Clarence Mooney shook his head in deprecation. "It came down to me when my brother died. I thought Ken might put the place in shape, get it going and make money for us all. But he just fiddled around."

"It's pretty far out in the hills," said Joe. "A long way to go for a beer."

"It's what people want nowadays," said Mooney. "Something old-fashioned. Look at 'em folk-dancing and folk-singing on TV. Like they got some kind of disease."

"If you've got a liquor license," said Joe, "that's worth money, maybe ten or twelve thousand."

"I realize that." When Clarence Mooney spoke of money a different note came into his voice: a reverent drone. Mrs. Mooney sat an inch straighter in her chair, the girls turned their eyes upward like young saints. "Yes indeed," Clarence Mooney droned. "There's twenty acres of land around the place. Ken wanted to sell the place for nothing. I wouldn't let him. Sooner or later I'll get my price."

"Maybe so. What's your price?"

"Just about forty…thousand…dollars." Mooney spoke the words slowly, quietly, as if they left a pleasant taste in his mouth.

"What did Ken want to do with the place?"

Clarence Mooney snorted. "That's something we could never get together on. He spent a little spare time out there, tinkered around, but he never gave it a real go. He just didn't have the *uch-uch-uch.*" Here Clarence Mooney, in synchronization with the curious sounds, made piston-like thrusts of arm and fist.

Joe, returning to the conjecture of blackmail as a background to the murder, suggested: "Ken had money put aside? Investments, something of the sort?"

"He saved his money, sure. But 'investment' —" Clarence Mooney jerked his thumb contemptuously toward the TV-stereophonic combination. "That's about the only investment he ever made. A present to Mother and the girls. And me."

"Hm. Nice."

Mrs. Mooney, whose attention had been momentarily diverted from the murder, crouched once more into her chair. The girls blinked and stiffened. Clarence Mooney grunted, turned away.

Joe rubbed his chin. So far, nothing. What to ask next? Somebody must know something, even if they didn't know they knew it. "Ken liked his work pretty well?"

"It was easy," said Clarence Mooney evenly.

"He lived here with you?"

"That's right."

"I'd like to look over his room, if you don't mind."

"This way."

"It's in a terrible mess," Mrs. Mooney called after them. "I didn't think to clean."

"Don't worry, Mother," said Clarence Mooney in a hollow voice.

They went to Ken's room, on the second floor, little more than a cubicle with a bed. Ken's wardrobe was nondescript; there was little to convey any sense of personality. On the wall hung two photographs of the Pleasant Grove High School football turnout: the entire squad, and the first team. Joe went to look at the pictures. Clarence Mooney indicated Ken, a muscular boy with a shock of dark hair hanging half down in his eyes. "There he is... Never think to look at him that things would turn out the way they did."

"You surely wouldn't."

"He was a real good boy." Clarence Mooney's voice again went hollow. "If I could catch hold of whoever did him in..." Clarence Mooney drew a deep breath. "I suppose it's foolish talking that way. I suppose it's foolish talking at all. People that's left alive have to go on living." He pointed to the quarterback, a keen-featured lad standing behind center, the lower half of his face split in a rather fatuous grin. "That's Bill Whipple. He went to college on one of them football deals. Ken played just as hard and good; do you think anybody gave him a lot of money? No sir. You don't get anywhere in this world unless you make a lot of noise. This is a noisy world." Clarence Mooney gave his gaunt hollow-eyed head a slow shake. "Out here on Oatfarm Road a man can scream bloody murder and nobody hears a sound."

"That's the way it goes," said Joe. He went to the wardrobe, felt through Ken's pockets, found a tube of lipstick and two dimes. The drawers in Ken's chiffonier yielded nothing. There were no letters, no diary, no personal papers. Ken was a young man who lived from day to day.

The older girl came shyly into the room with a photograph album and Ken's high school year-book. Joe saw Ken at all stages of his life: baby, toddler, small boy, youth, and man. In the year-book the girl pointed out more pictures of Ken. Joe studied a snapshot of Ken kneeling on a flight of steps with two pretty girls beside him. "Love to Ken" was written across the picture in a neat girlish handwriting, and there were two signatures: 'Alice Benjamin', 'Barbara Duncan'.

Joe put an ingenuous question: "Were these his girl friends?"

Ken's sister smiled quickly, nervously. "Not really. Ken never went steady. He took out all different girls."

"He never liked any special girls?"

"He said he liked them all, and couldn't make up his mind."

Joe went downstairs. Mrs. Mooney had not moved from her chair. The younger girl had turned on the television set, but reception was poor and little could be seen but flickering films of green and red and ghostly orange shapes.

Joe departed the somber house. As he drove south down Oatfarm Road the hills seemed peculiarly free and wild, and the land spreading to the west seemed open, boundless, unconstrained. "I guess I'm becoming a nature lover, or maybe a bird watcher," Joe muttered to himself. "It's a relief to get out of that house."

3

Returning to his office, Joe found Miss Curdy arguing with an old Mexican woman.

"¿Que paso?" inquired Joe. "What goes on?"

"She wants to see one of the prisoners," said Miss Curdy. "It's out of visiting hours. I told her no."

"¡Si, si, si! Quiero hablar a Juan Carminez. ¡Es muy importante!"

"¿Porque importante?" Joe asked.

"Su hijo está en el hospital. Muy enfermo."

"Wait a minute," said Joe. He looked into the back room. "Where's Lew Gonzalez?" he asked Ace Wardell.

"Out on patrol."

"Rats. Does anybody around here speak Spanish better than I do?"

"There's Carminez back in the zoo."

Joe took the keys, unlocked the gate, brought Carminez out. "Lady here wants to talk to you, something about your son."

Carminez went to the front desk. There was a staccato interchange. Carminez turned to Joe. "She says my boy is sick. Appendicitis. He wants to see me. Maybe I better go."

"Maybe you better not go. This is a jail, not a hotel."

"But Sheriff! He's just a little boy!"

"Too bad," said Joe. "You should have thought of that before you began stabbing that man."

Carminez looked at Joe in angry reproach. "I didn't know my boy was going to be sick! Maybe he dies now!"

"He's not going to die," said Joe. "It's just appendicitis. There's three men off, nobody on standby. I can't spare anybody to take you out... All right, go on out, see your boy. You get back here fast, you hear?"

"Yes, Sheriff."

"I want you back by six o'clock. What hospital is it?"

"County Hospital."

"All right then. Six o'clock."

"Okay, Sheriff, thanks. I'll be back pretty soon."

"Damn betcha."

Joe walked back to his office. Ace Wardell leaned out of his glass-paneled booth. "What goes on?"

"Some kind of Mexican jail break. Miss Curdy thinks I'm insane. What the hell."

"Is he coming back?"

"I can't worry about that right now. Too many Mexicans in jail anyway. We'll never miss an odd one or two. Try to get hold of Kelly."

Ace spoke into the microphone, elicited a rasp of response and reported to Joe. "He's on his way in."

Joe went into his office, put his feet up on the desk. Ken Mooney, an apparently inoffensive mail carrier, had been killed. Why? How? Joe put through a call to Dr. Hesketh. "Sheriff Joe Bain, Doctor. Anything interesting on Ken Mooney?"

"Nothing much. Time remains the same: around ten o'clock yesterday, give or take an hour. First whack probably killed him. I'd say the blows were struck with an ordinary sixteen-ounce carpenter's hammer. Three smart blows. No rage or frenzy. Just three good raps."

"Alcohol? Drugs?"

"Nothing shows up. Organs all in good shape. He didn't even smoke."

"What about blood? There wasn't much in the van."

"He didn't bleed much. A blow like the one that killed him — well, let's say it pushes a plug of bone and tissue into the brain. The heart stops; there's a certain amount of seepage from the ruptured blood vessels of the epidermis — but no great puddle."

"That *Life* magazine now —" here Joe, with a pang, thought of a line of investigation he had neglected "— you think that might have absorbed all of the bleeding?"

"Yes, I'd say so. I wouldn't swear to it in court."

"Thank you, Doctor." Joe cradled the phone. He took the torpedo-shaped pen from the black onyx desk set which had been his birthday present from Miranda, and wrote on a blank sheet of paper:

KEN MOONEY
Check Life subscriptions along Madrone Way.
Check for hammers, test for blood.

It was a peculiar business, thought Joe — up to now, anyway. According to Henry Deardorf and Clarence Mooney Ken had not an enemy in the world — which just went to show that things weren't always what they seemed. Ken had at least one enemy.

Bill Whipple? The name leapt to mind. Bill lived on Madrone Way; he was one of Ken's associates. Joe grimaced, as if at a bad taste. Bill Whipple as a hammer murderer didn't seem reasonable, even though he didn't know Bill Whipple.

Well then, who?

That was the question, thought Joe.

He sat musing until Rex Kelly made his appearance. Kelly was a tall young man with a square amiable face, thick crew-cut brown hair. Joe considered him far and away the best man on his staff, even though he lacked experience. Kelly was college trained; he was intelligent, friendly with the public, hardworking. His single lack — drive? initiative? — was a quality which made him a good subordinate. Joe dreaded the day when Rex Kelly became dissatisfied with his job and went looking for something better. Hard-working intelligent deputies were not to be found under every bush.

Kelly had visited every house along Madrone Way. "I tried the Shortridge place first. The mailbox is just inside the driveway; usually the carrier shoves the mail in the box. Yesterday there was a C.O.D. package. Ken collected from Marsh Shortridge, who happened to be home. Starr was also at home. Mr. Sam Shortridge was at the store, Mrs. Miriam Shortridge was at her hairdresser's. Starr claims not to have seen Ken. She says she was reading a book. Marsh paid for the package, talked with Ken about half a minute, then Ken drove off down the driveway. Marsh saw nothing suspicious, no rider in the van. Ken seemed in good spirits. Nobody at the Shortridge house has any theories or any remarks to make. Starr is either cold-blooded or remote or plain snooty: I can't figure her out. Attractive girl, if you can take the supercilious expression. Marsh is getting married in a month or so to a girl up the street. A rather lofty fellow, wouldn't admit to knowing Ken, spoke of him as 'the mailman'.

"Next house: residents are Thomas and Betty Taylor and four small boys. Taylor is president of Valley Savings and Loan. I talked to Mrs. Taylor. She did not see Ken. He dropped mail in the box, drove on.

"Third house, the Benjamin residence. Guy Benjamin is a civil engineer, in India on an eighteen-month contract. Mrs. Grace Benjamin is quite pregnant. She's 40 if she's a day. Frozen-faced woman. Marsh Shortridge is marrying her daughter Alice. I don't envy him his mother-in-law. Alice is in Europe and won't be back for another month or so. Mrs. Benjamin admits to knowing Ken by sight, but speaks of him disapprovingly — too familiar, too forward. She's got madonnas and crucifixes backwards and forwards through the house, a hard-nose Catholic. Ken dropped the mail in her box without her seeing him.

"Next door is Mrs. Sally Wagner, about 37 or 38, not bad-looking, a little plump maybe. She'll talk your ear off. This is the place to go for gossip. She's divorced — ex-husband lives in Beverly Hills. My guess is that she's living on alimony. She knows Ken and considers his death a terrible tragedy. She says he was 'honest and genuine, a very sweet boy'. She didn't see him yesterday. He pushed the mail through the slot in her door and was gone. She thinks Ken must have been killed by a thief.

"Next door, Fred and Sheila Whipple, their son Bill. Fred was at work Tuesday morning. Sheila says that when she saw Ken she generally said hello because he was a friend of Bill's. Tuesday morning she only caught a glimpse of him, and he seemed in a terrible hurry. She's a pretty sharp woman, not much education, I'd say, and a trifle bitter with her neighbors along Madrone Way. I guess they haven't given the Whipples a grand welcome. Bill is a student at San Jose State, working the summer for Whipple Chevrolet, on the used car lot. Mrs. Whipple can't imagine who would want to kill Ken; she says Bill is just as puzzled. I didn't talk to either Fred Whipple or Bill.

"Next, Milo Gentry's house. Gentry is one of the county supervisors. I guess you know that. He and Mrs. Gentry are visiting their grandchildren in Montana; the house is empty except for the housekeeper, an old colored lady who says she never pays any attention to the mailman. She didn't even know he was dead until I told her. She saw nothing suspicious or peculiar.

"Next door is the high school principal and his wife: Caspar Hubman, Laura Hubman. I talked to him ten minutes before he'd even admit to being alive. Pompous brute, figures himself for an intellectual. He won't state whether or not he knows Ken, says the question is meaningless. He claims that as an educator he knows two-thirds the population of Pleasant Grove; as a private citizen he knows no one. So take your choice. My feeling is that he knew Ken well enough, but doesn't want to get involved. His wife is one of these arty types — weaves rugs and makes pots. Incidentally the wife is Mrs. Bazzarini's daughter, which may be where the money comes from. They have an elegant house. It's not too big — there aren't any children — but it's full of nice things. Mrs. Hubman is easier to talk to than Caspar the educator, but she's slick as oil. She says she knew Ken to say hello to but after all he was only the mailman, and she knew nothing about his private life. Neither Caspar nor Laura saw or heard anything suspicious Tuesday morning. Caspar was writing a book; Laura was potting some plants. It's possible that either could have bashed Ken.

"Next door is the Mortimer house, closed up tight as a drum. If Ken surprised a burglar, it was a burglar so inefficient as to be unbelievable."

Joe interposed a question. "Suppose the burglar was some marauding kid? Not a pro, but some young hoodlum maybe fourteen or fifteen?"

Rex Kelly shrugged. "Possible. At the Mortimer house Ken stopped delivering mail, which must mean something. I checked the grounds pretty carefully — and there isn't a dandelion out of place. I can try again if you like. Anyway, on to Mrs. Bazzarini. She's alone in the house except for her nurses and her dog. There once was a son, but he got killed in an automobile accident. She doesn't seem to like the Hubmans very much, but she certainly liked Ken. He made it a habit to come in and talk with her. She claims she knew all about him — his family, girl friends, ambitions. She can't imagine why anyone would want to kill him — which is what all the rest say."

"Okay, Rex, good work," said Joe. "Looks like we've got two possibilities. After Ken delivered to the Mortimer house, he was either persuaded to drive away from Madrone Way, or he was killed by someone along Madrone Way. Now thinking about that *Life* magazine. It seems like the murderer put it under Ken's head to catch the blood, then tore the label off to keep us from learning his name. If the label wasn't important, he wouldn't bother to tear it off. Here's what I want you to do. Start along Madrone Way, find out which families subscribe to *Life* and ask to see the current copy. Say you want to eliminate their names from the list of theoretical possibilities, keep 'em happy the best way you can. Right now I'll call Deardorf. The magazines in Ken's van will no doubt go out in tomorrow's delivery. I'll have him ask the carrier to check the remainder of Ken's route. He might have to make a list of the addresses and check them off against next week's delivery. Eventually we'll find if the murderer used his own magazine or snatched one at random.

"Secondly: Doc Hesketh thinks the weapon might be a hammer — a common carpenter's hammer. Ask the people along Madrone Way if you can check on their hammers. Be gentle: tell them you know they're not guilty, but you suspect that their hammer might have been stolen. Collect the hammers, label them, bring them back and we'll give them the blood test. We might just turn up something. Got all that?"

"Right. *Life* magazines; check on hammers."

"Don't accuse any important people. I want to stay sheriff awhile."

Rex Kelly departed. Joe telephoned the post office and was connected with Henry Deardorf. "Hello, Mr. Deardorf. Sheriff Joe Bain here."

"Yes, Sheriff; what have you learned?"

"We're accumulating facts. You can help me out in regard to that *Life* which was under Ken's head. I want to find out where it was delivered."

"I can't help you there. The label was torn off."

"This is what I want you to do. Tomorrow you'll deliver the mail left in Ken's van. Ask the carrier to check along the route when he makes delivery, to find if anyone is missing a magazine. Have him list the addresses on the magazines which were left in the van, then next week we'll check off the new batch against this list."

"What's that again?" asked Deardorf suspiciously. Joe explained a second time, and Deardorf agreed to instruct his carrier.

"Incidentally," said Deardorf, "a somewhat curious situation has come up. I don't quite understand it."

"Yes, Mr. Deardorf?"

"We checked the registered mail against our tally book; everything was regular. But one of these items of registered mail was for Mrs. Benjamin which Mooney did not deliver."

"Eh? Come again."

"There was a registered letter for Mrs. Benjamin. Mooney delivered the other mail, but not the registered letter, which of course is highly irregular."

"Could he maybe have been worried about something and forgot it?"

"No sir. There's a yellow ticket the carrier puts into the bundle, so that he won't forget."

"Hmm," said Joe. "I'll give the matter some thought. All these peculiar odds and ends must mean something."

"I certainly hope you're right."

The conversation ended. Joe leaned back in his chair and tried to think rationally. Who stood to profit from Ken's death? He had no money, he owned no property, not even Halfway House. Blackmail? Unlikely, if the general estimate of Ken's character were correct. A crime of passion? More likely a jealous husband than a love-crazed woman. Had the mail carrier been killed by mistake? Every conceivable reason for Ken's death seemed far-fetched. Still — a corpse existed.

Joe tried to decide what to do next. Rex Kelly was checking on the *Life* and the hammer. Bill Whipple was the most important next step. Joe called Whipple Chevrolet, but was told Mr. Bill Whipple was not on hand.

Joe called the Whipple residence and learned that Bill was not at home either.

Hanging up the receiver Joe stared despondently across the room. The case had all the earmarks of an enormous headache; and there was no place to hide. A murder had been committed, Sheriff Joe Bain was now expected to apprehend the evil-doer. Joe felt like an actor with stage-fright. After solving the Fox Valley murders he had been hailed as a super-criminologist, a deductive genius: compliments which he had modestly shrugged aside. Howard Griselda, editor and publisher of the *Pleasant Grove Messenger*, had not participated in the congratulations. Griselda, a dour and busy-browed Scot, played the role of country editor to the hilt. With Howard Griselda, courageous hard-hitting editorials, crusades and campaigns were a way of life. Griselda suspected Joe of ethical relativism and about now he would be puffing vigorously on his pipe, theorizing how best the murder of Ken Mooney might be attributed to improprieties at the sheriff's office.

Joe nervously ran his hands through his black hair. It was a case of produce or else.

He looked at his watch: four-thirty in the afternoon. One department of Ken Mooney's life remained to be explored: Halfway House.

Joe informed Ace Wardell of his destination, politely told Miss Curdy that he was leaving for the day. She seemed even more terse than usual — still brooding over the furlough extended Juan Carminez, thought Joe. Well, let her brood, so long as she got her work done. If she didn't like it, she could run for sheriff herself at the next election.

CHAPTER V

1

JOE DROVE WEST toward Jordan. Ten miles from town Contreras Road led off through the foothills — a section of the old coach-road joining Monterey to Vallejo and Sonoma. For a mile or two Contreras Creek paralleled the road, then swung off to the south to join Genesee Creek. The road plunged into a dense redwood forest which for a space blocked out the sunlight. Then the forest thinned somewhat, a graveled driveway turned off to the right, and there, a hundred feet back from the road, was Halfway House, a sprawling old-fashioned structure of redwood and stone. Posts rose from the first-floor porch to support a second-story balcony where hung a faded old black and gold sign:

HALFWAY HOUSE
Historic Coach Stop
Beers — Wines — Ales
GOOD FOOD
ACCOMMODATION

Three sets of double doors opened on the porch, but only the doors to the bar showed signs of recent usage. Joe climbed out of the car, looked the place over. The structure was run-down certainly, but nothing that money and elbow-grease wouldn't make right. Joe wondered if maybe Clarence Mooney's appraisal of his son's character wasn't accurate. If he, Joe, owned an old place like this, he'd give it loving care, really put it back into shape. The stained-glass panels in the doors, for instance: those were high-quality items, dating from the turn of the century. The place wasn't just a shack ...

From around the back of the building came a stout old man with a grizzled bulldog face. He wore snuff-colored trousers, a tan sportshirt, a battered fiber hat. He looked at the black and white official car and came forward. "Hi there. You the sheriff or the deputy?"

"I'm Sheriff Joe Bain."

"Pleased to meetcha. I'm Wilbur Baker, caretaker around here."

The two men shook hands.

"Nice old place," said Joe. "I guess it doesn't do much business."

"Nope. No more. I guess you'd say she's closed up. Maybe for good. I had some good times out here during Prohibition. I was just a kid then."

"Before my time," said Joe. "You've been working for Ken Mooney, I take it."

"Just helpin' out. Last year I kept the bar open, made enough to buy my beans. But —" he shook his head "— I got fed up. I don't know what Ken figures to do. Nice boy and all that, but he can't seem to get himself pointed straight." Wilbur Baker glanced sidewise at the official car. "What brings you out this way, Sheriff?"

"I'm investigating a homicide," said Joe. "Matter of fact, Ken Mooney got himself killed."

Wilbur Baker stared round-eyed. "You mean — Ken? He's dead?"

"Dead as a doornail."

"Well I never," breathed Wilbur Baker. "What do you know about that? Who did it?"

"I don't know," said Joe. "Doesn't seem to be any rhyme or reason to the case. I thought I'd come out here, ask a few questions."

"Why certainly. I must say I'm shocked. Fancy that! Ken! Just what happened?"

"He was hit over the head with a hammer. It appears that one of his friends did the job."

Wilbur Baker uttered an expletive. "That's not much of a friend!"

"Did you know any of his friends?"

"No sir, I did not. Ken was out of my generation. I'll say this, he treated me right. He was easy to get along with; more so than me, most likely."

"Ken came out here pretty often?"

Wilbur Baker squinted in thought. "When Charley Mooney first died, he came out quite a bit. He wanted to furbish up the place, get it going again. But he never could raise the money. For a while he was out every weekend. He hauled away junk, painted, reglazed windows, fixed up the dance floor. He even put a big new mirror behind the bar. That cost him a pretty penny, and he worked like a beaver: Ken and one of his friends."

"Who was the friend?"

"Bill somebody. Kind of reckless-looking young fellow. Acted pretty know-it-all. He bossed the job, told Ken what to do, how to do it, bawled him out when Ken didn't move to suit him. It put my back up. I turned right around and left."

"This Bill — is he the only one of Ken's friends who helped him?"

"Yeah, I'd say so. During the past six months Ken didn't come out too much — maybe two or three times. I guess he just plain ran out of gas."

Joe glanced at his watch. He wanted to be home for dinner. "I'd like to take a look inside, if it's all right with you."

Wilbur Baker shrugged. "Certainly it's all right with me, if you think it'll help."

"You never know in this business."

They climbed stone steps to the porch. Wilbur Baker unlocked a padlock, pushed open double doors. They entered the bar. Mahogany glimmered through the gloom. On the wall shone Ken's impressive new mirror. Everywhere were mementoes, old photographs, curios. The room had a pleasant odor; a redolence of old wood, old varnish, antique whiskey, evaporated beer. Impalpable echoes hung in the air: the ghosts of dead music and dead laughter; a fairy tinkle of ice and glassware. Joe drew a deep breath, shook his head. These old places drew him, filled him with nostalgia for the good old times. Here at Halfway House there was more. The place wasn't dead. There was still vitality here; the place was waiting to come back to life. Joe could imagine cars parked in front of the porch, colored lights twinkling above the dance floor, maybe a four-piece band with people dancing.

On the floor beside the front wall was a case containing a dozen empty champagne bottles. Joe said to Wilbur Baker, "Seems like you have expensive tastes."

"What do you mean? Oh. That stuff. Not me. I don't drink. That's the remains of a party Ken had out here last fall. No, by golly. It was closer to Christmas. He brought out his girl friend — pretty little thing, my yes — and another couple. They built a big fire and drank that wine and caroused most of the night. Who knows what-all went on. I wasn't invited."

"Hm. Did Ken have many parties like that?"

"Nothing like that one."

"Who was the other fellow? This 'Bill' you mentioned?"

"That's right. But don't think I paid them any heed. You'd be surprised how I mind my own business."

"That's the sensible way to be," said Joe. "But right now I wish you had been just a bit nosier."

He looked into the dining room and the lobby beyond. Upstairs, according to Wilbur Baker, were ten bedrooms and two baths. Joe wanted to investigate more thoroughly, but the sun had dropped behind the mountains and the hour was getting late.

Joe went out into the front yard, and stood looking the old place over. Was it worth forty thousand dollars? Maybe not. It needed a lot of work: new plumbing, new wiring, new furniture, probably a modern kitchen. That kind of equipment cost money. Joe made a mental calculation. There were twenty acres of land, worth, say, four thousand dollars. Liquor license worth ten or twelve. That put the value of the structure at about twenty-five thousand. Joe grimaced dubiously. For a fact the building couldn't be replaced for that amount, not using sound materials, the way it used to be done. The curse of the age: cheap materials, cheap thinking, cheap people. Everything was cheap nowadays. Go into a supermarket: red lights shone on the meat; there was loudspeaker music to send you jigging through the aisles, throwing caution to the winds. Not to mention the breweries and their eleven-ounce cans of beer to cheat a man out of his last swallow. In the old days when the robber barons took your gold, it was honest brigandage; there were no hard feelings. Stealing nowadays was so small, so petty, so hypocritical. The corporations used one hand to pick your pocket, the other to scratch your back. They called it their 'public image'. Well, it had nothing to do with him. When the judge said, "Thirty days," Joe saw to it that the man got a full thirty days: his money's worth, so to speak … At least this was usually what Joe did. He wondered if Carminez had returned to jail yet. With good luck Howard Griselda might not hear about the incident … Joe got into his car. Tomorrow or the next day he'd give the place a more careful examination, look through the kitchen and the bedrooms. It seemed a comfortable old place. But forty thousand dollars' worth? Yes — for a wealthy antiquarian. Forty thousand dollars would buy a lot of romance. Unlikely that Clarence Mooney knew the meaning of the word. The place might be a good buy at twenty-five thousand, thought Joe. If he had twenty-five thousand he might consider making an offer. Ridiculous thought … He called out to Wilbur Baker: "I'll be going on. If you think of anything, give me a call."

Wilbur Baker came forward rubbing his stubbled chin. "I don't have any standing here now that Ken's dead. I suppose I'll stay on until somebody tells me to leave."

"Ken's father has title to the place," said Joe. "He'll probably be getting in touch with you."

2

The drive back to Pleasant Grove was like a trip from one world to another. At Halfway House even Ken Mooney's murder had seemed remote and theoretical … Joe remembered Juan Carminez and radioed headquarters. Juan Carminez had not reported back to jail, and Miss Curdy had been making sarcastic remarks.

"Tell Miss Curdy to go jump in the lake," said Joe.

"You tell her," said Ace Wardell. "You're Sheriff, not me … Here comes Carminez now. Good God! What a mess. He's been through the wars."

"I'll be there in fifteen minutes. Call home for me, say I've been detained."

"Right."

When Joe returned to headquarters Carminez was back in his cell. Miss Curdy, just preparing to leave for the night, was speaking into the telephone: "— Juan Carminez? He's here, in his cell. Certainly I'm sure. He just —"

Joe, across the room with one bound, took the receiver from Miss Curdy's stiff fingers. "Sheriff Bain speaking. What's the trouble?"

An excited female voice sputtered into his ear. "They say it was Juan Carminez hit my son; I say no, Carminez is in jail. They say no, by golly, it looks like Juan. I want to know, is Juan Carminez in jail or not?"

"Juan Carminez is in his cell," declared Joe. "What happened?"

"I don't know. They call me from La Fiesta; you know that place?"

"Yeah," said Joe in a hollow voice. "I know the place."

"They say Carminez comes in, he looks around, he goes over and hits my son. If it isn't Carminez, who is it?"

"Well, ma'am, I can sure investigate. Do you want to swear out a warrant against Juan Carminez and take him to court?"

There was silence. Then cautiously: "You say he's in jail?"

"He sure is, Cell 10. Come down and see for yourself."

"Then who hit my son?"

"Are there any witnesses?"

The voice became excited again. "My boy say it's Juan. He say Juan Carminez come up and hits him and say 'You son-of-a-bitch, how do you like that?' And my boy hits Carminez and he says 'How do you like that?' And then Juan Carminez hits my boy with a big toy truck made out of plastic, and he say 'How do you like that?' And then he goes away."

"I see. Your son identifies Juan Carminez?"

"He says it's Juan Carminez."

"What is your son's name?"

"Ramon Aguilar."

"Send him down to the jail. I'll show him Juan Carminez sitting in Cell 10."

Another short silence.

Joe asked politely, "Had your son been drinking, Mrs. Aguilar?"

"Yes, maybe. I tell him it don't do no good. He drinks beer and whiskey all the time, I can't make him stop. It's bad for him, costs him money; he don't stop."

"You tell him Sheriff Joe Bain says he better stop boozing; he might find himself in the next cell to Juan Carminez."

"Okay, Sheriff. I tell him. He's not real bad, just takes a drink of beer."

Joe hung up. Miss Curdy stood watching with an unfathomable expression. Joe shook his head in gloomy disgust, marched back to the jail. Juan Carminez looked at him through the bars.

"How was your sick boy, Juan?" asked Joe.

"I guess he's all right, Sheriff. He was pretty sick."

"Sure a funny situation. Mrs. Aguilar says a man that looks like you hit her son Ramon with a toy plastic truck."

Carminez' mouth drooped wistfully. "Maybe she made a mistake."

"All I can say, Juan, is that you sure made a donkey out of both of us. Miss Curdy thinks I'm insane, Mrs. Aguilar thinks I'm running a holiday resort. She wants me to tie you up with big chains so you can't hit her son Ramon any more."

Juan managed a sick smile. "Don't believe what they tell you. That Ramon Aguilar, he's trying to get me in trouble."

"Yeah, maybe so. Well, Juan, I'm sure disappointed in you. Tomorrow I'm going to ask Miss Curdy to come in and talk to you."

"Don't worry, Sheriff, don't go to no trouble. I'm a pretty good guy."

"I'm glad to hear that. I want you to spend the night thinking good thoughts. I want you to pray that Ramon Aguilar's head doesn't hurt too bad. I want you to put on that look of injured innocence when Howard Griselda appears."

Juan Carminez shrugged, acquiescent to any or all of Sheriff Bain's whims. "Just like you say, Sheriff."

Joe went home, slumped down in an old wicker chair with a can of beer. From the kitchen came the odor of corned beef and cabbage, from the bathroom the sounds of the shower mingled with the catarrhal bleat of a popular vocal quartet: an exasperating sound, but by some paradox, soothing. Here, if nowhere else in the world, was normality.

Joe consumed a second can of beer, and even the murder of Ken Mooney seemed less disturbing. Puzzling, perplexing, to be sure; but nothing to get hysterical about. In due course the elements of the situation would line up to form a pattern, and Joe would make an arrest.

Joe popped the lid on a third can of beer, in spite of Marian Bain's glance of admonishment. "I'm serving a nice dinner in three minutes," she told him, "and I don't want you coming to the table sozzled. Your father was bad enough."

"'Sozzled'? On a couple cans of beer? Ridiculous."

"Three cans of beer and heaven knows how much more downtown. Miranda! Dinner's on the table…Miranda, what are you doing?"

"Putting on my clothes. Do you want me to come in a towel?"

"Hurry up. Goodness, I forgot the horseradish. Your father will have a fit."

After a few minutes Miranda rather saucily asked Joe what was new and interesting.

"Oh, not much," said Joe. "Just a killing. You probably never knew the corpse; he'd be several years ahead of you at school."

"Who?"

"Young fellow named Ken Mooney."

"There's a Mooney girl who's a freshman. She'll be a sophomore next year."

"That's his sister."

"Oh. Too bad. Who killed him?"

"I wish I knew. You probably know Alice Benjamin and Starr Shortridge."

"I know who they are," said Miranda. "They were two years ahead of me."

Marian Bain asked, "You don't mean the Shortridge family is involved?"

"I don't mean anything. I don't know anything. But I'll find out."

"You always were the most persistent boy," said Marian Bain. "I'll never forget the time you wanted a bicycle and cracked all those black walnuts."

"I never did get it."

"Your dad was a rascal, no doubt about it. But he had his good points too."

"Trying to fill an inside straight wasn't one of them. In fact they say that's what got him killed."

Marian Bain made disapproving noises. Joe wasn't supposed to talk about the knifing of Blacky Bain in front of Miranda.

"Well, that's all in the past," said Joe. "How'd you girls like to run an old-fashioned hotel?"

"What do you mean?"

"I stopped by Halfway House out on Contreras Road today. It's up for sale."

"You're joking," said Marian Bain. "I'm sure you're joking."

"I suppose I am. It's a real nice old place, on twenty acres of big red-woods. It needs work — mainly cleaning and new glass, new curtains, new furniture, things like that."

"Who'd want to go out to Contreras Road to sleep?" inquired Marian Bain. "Why wouldn't they stay home?"

"People down from San Francisco and San Jose. Old country hotels are going big nowadays, especially if there's a liquor license."

Marian Bain shook her head. "I've seen all the drinking I ever want to see."

"Oh Granny!" protested Miranda. "It's just an old country hotel. I've driven past there. It's got an old dining room, bedrooms looking out on the balcony. It looks like a real fun place. Suppose we had horses and a swimming pool and a tennis court."

"Yeah," said Joe. "And a golf course and speedboats and a ferris wheel."

"Now you're being silly, Daddy."

"He certainly is," declared Marian Bain.

"It's not impossible," argued Joe. "It's an investment. I figured you two would run the place. We'd hire a bartender, of course."

"Granny could tend bar," said Miranda slyly. "I'd be bar girl."

"I should say not! All that drinking and carousing? I wouldn't think of it. And it's certainly no place to bring up a young girl."

"I'm not all that young! Think! You could serve corned beef and cabbage and make wild blackberry pies."

"I think it would go over," said Joe. "People like to come to some quiet place and do nothing but loaf. No juke-box, no TV, maybe a Sat-urday night dance, but nothing else."

Marian Bain smiled wistfully. "That's the way things used to be when I was a girl. I'll never forget when I was about ten or eleven we made a trip to Idaho and stayed at some of the nicest old places. It makes me sad just to think of them. They're all torn down now, I expect."

"Halfway House is the same kind of old hotel. It just needs a lot of hard work to get it in operation."

Marian Bain pursed her lips. "I'm not afraid of hard work, you know that very well. But I'd want to look the place over before I'd even think about it. It could wear a person out."

"I'd work," said Miranda. "I'd love it. I'd even get my friends to help. They'd love it too. It would be *fun*!"

"I can imagine the kind of help your friends would be," snapped Marian Bain. "Especially that Gilpepper boy. I don't trust him. He's got a funny shifty look."

"Oh Granny! Warren is tiresome but he's nice. He can beat me at chess. He beats everybody at chess."

"Chess will never make him a living. What is this place going for, Joe?"

"The man wants forty thousand dollars."

Marian Bain leaned back aghast, her eyes large and round. "Forty thousand dollars? And you're the man who's been preaching economy to me and Miranda? How can you even think about spending so much money? Even if you had it?"

"That's what banks are for," said Joe. "I'm Sheriff now, miserably underpaid even after a raise. Still, twelve hundred a month is better than nothing."

"It's more than your father and I would see in a year."

"Another thing," said Joe, "I don't plan to spend forty thousand dollars. Clarence Mooney will dance for joy if I mention, say, twenty-five."

"It seems very rash, Joe, when things are going so nicely —"

"Heavens, I thought you were aching to get away from this old house!"

"Well, in a way. But I was thinking of another house, not a wild scheme as bad as any of your father's. You're like him in so many ways."

"Daddy, let's go out and look at the place. Can we?"

"Tonight?"

"Right now."

"See if your grandmother wants to go."

"Oh, I'll go for the ride. But don't expect me to walk all around this hour of the night."

"Good enough," said Joe. "Let's go."

3

Wilbur Baker came rather grumpily out of his shack, opened the door, threw on the main power switch. "Just pull the switch and lock up when you leave. I'm going back to bed."

"Thanks very much, Mr. Baker."

Miranda walked into the bar, looked around in entrancement. "This is just like the twenties. You can just see people dancing the Charleston and the shimmy."

"Your grandmother would know more about that than I would. I understand she used to do a pretty fancy cake-walk."

"I never did," snorted Marian Bain. "That was old even in my day. We danced the fox trot and the waltz, and the tango too. I was a very good dancer. You'd never know it to look at me now, of course."

"Waltz out here into the kitchen," said Joe. "It doesn't seem too bad. It's even clean."

"I'm surprised," said Marian Bain. "Really surprised. Is that a wood range? I believe it is. I don't see any refrigerator."

"We'd put in modern equipment," said Joe. "Also some new floor tile."

"That's not hard," said Miranda. "I can do that myself. I think yellow and white would be perfect. And I'd paint the walls yellow too. And the ceiling pale blue."

"Dark brown is more practical," said Joe. "It doesn't show the dirt."

Marian Bain swung around in shock. "You're the first person that has ever accused me of having a dirty kitchen."

"No, no! I didn't accuse you. I just said that if there happened to be dirt —"

"Never mind. Just don't think you'll paint any kitchen of mine dark brown, or black either. My, look at those big windows. It would be a lovely place for my African violets."

Miranda had run into the dining room. "It's nothing very fancy," she said when Joe and his mother followed her. "I think we should use blue- and red-checkered tablecloths and candles, like the Isola Bella in Monterey. I'd paint the walls white in here, I think. And hang up some pictures. Picassos would be nice."

"Be reasonable," said Joe. "We want people to eat."

"Daddy, you're a barbarian. You don't have any artistic sense at all."

"Maybe not…The lobby is through here, girls."

Miranda, going behind the desk, found a dusty old register. "Look at this! It goes back ages!" She flipped back through the years. "1930 — 1928 — 1924. Here's the page for Saturday, July 21, 1924. 'Mr. and Mrs. Albert Hall, Walnut Creek', 'Mr. and Mrs. Henry Jones, San Francisco', 'Mr. and Mrs. William Clark, San Jose', 'Mr. and Mrs. John Wilson, Oakland'."

Joe grinned. "Lots of Joneses and Smiths and Wilsons." He turned the pages of the register forward, to the last entry, which was dated December 19 of the year previous: *Ken Mooney and* — here there was a scrawl as if someone had snatched the pen from his hand and then had scribbled *Theda Bara.*

Underneath someone else had written: *Rudolph Valentino and Mae Murray.*

Joe scrutinized the signatures. "Looks like Ken's friends have a lively sense of humor."

"He must have had a party here," Miranda decided.

"That's what it looks like," said Joe. "A pretty elegant affair, to judge from all the champagne they drank." He turned back through the pages, but found nothing more to interest him. His mother decided that she had seen enough and they presently went out to the car.

"Well, what do you think?" Joe asked his mother.

"I can't tell you what to do. It's your money, your responsibility."

"I know it. But you'd have to take charge of the place. I couldn't run it."

"Well…let's not do anything rash. I think you should look into the place a little more carefully."

Miranda said in a casual voice, "I'd probably have to have a car to get to school in, but we need another car anyway. Maybe a Volkswagen, or a —"

"I knew there was a fly in the ointment," said Marian Bain.

"There's a school bus that passes nearby," said Joe. "Probably right down Contreras Road."

"Those stupid old buses," complained Miranda. "Only creeps and little kids ride buses. Everybody else drives their own car."

Joe asked, "Aren't you one of the pace-setters? Start a new style. Make automobiles disreputable."

"But I *need* a car!"

"Yeah, about like I need a wife."

"Oh Daddy!" said Miranda in utter disgust.

"Don't worry, Miranda," sniffed Marian Bain. "He's not even divorced from his last wife yet."

"My *last* wife? My *first* wife!"

"I don't see what it's got to do with my having a car," Miranda said.

"In the first place you're too young. In the second place it's too dangerous and it costs too much. In the third place I put my foot down. In the fourth place you don't need a car since chances are this Halfway House talk is just an idle dream."

Miranda sat in sullen silence. Marian Bain asked presently, "Just who owns Halfway House, or did you say?"

"I mentioned Ken Mooney, the young fellow that had his head beat in. Well, the property is in his family."

"Hmmf…Who do you think killed the boy?"

"I haven't the slightest idea. The more I think the more confused I get. To preserve my sanity I've stopped thinking."

"I wish you'd be serious once in a while."

"I *am* serious. This case is a mystery. Tomorrow I've got to do some real digging, unfortunately among all the big shots. I'm not looking forward to it. Maybe I'll assign Miss Curdy to the job. When you grow up and get pinched, Miranda, don't get sent to Tehachapi; Miss Curdy is one of the drop-outs. The first team must be something to see."

"If Miss Curdy is so awful, why don't you fire her?" asked Marian Bain.

"I don't have anybody else for the job. What about you? There's not much to it except writing vouchers and searching drunk females, maybe giving 'em a clout or two."

"The very idea!"

Joe grinned. "I guess Miss Curdy's job is secure."

Chapter VI

1

ON THE FOLLOWING MORNING Joe set forth to interrogate the residents of Madrone Way.

The Shortridge home sat a hundred yards back from the road at the top of an S-shaped driveway. Miriam Shortridge herself answered the doorbell. "Yes?"

"Mrs. Shortridge? I'm Sheriff Joe Bain. May I come in?"

"Of course. I suppose you're investigating the murder." Mrs. Shortridge led the way into a vast living room decorated in that style known as French Provincial. "Please sit down."

She was perhaps fifty years old, a handsome woman who clearly devoted much effort to her appearance. Her hair was carefully coiffed; her skin was soft and clear; her manner was correct but not cordial.

"What I'd like you to tell me, Mrs. Shortridge, is everything you know which might have some conceivable bearing on the situation," said Joe. "For instance, did you ever notice Ken Mooney talking to anyone along the street? Did he ever make any kind of peculiar remark to you? Anything you can tell me might be helpful."

"I was not acquainted with the poor man," said Mrs. Shortridge. "I know nothing whatever either about him or the circumstances of his death."

"I hardly expected that you would," said Joe. "But occasionally an observant person just happens to notice something which strikes him as being out of the ordinary."

"I'm sorry. There's nothing I can tell you."

"Was your son or daughter acquainted with Ken Mooney?"

"I think you'd better ask them."

"You don't know?"

"I think Marshall knew Ken Mooney at high school, and probably Starr also. I don't imagine that either Marshall or Starr considered Ken Mooney a friend."

"I understand that on Tuesday morning Mr. Shortridge was working at the store and that you were at the beauty salon."

"I was visiting the hairdresser," said Mrs. Shortridge in a flat voice. "Mr. Shortridge was at his office."

"Do you subscribe to *Life* magazine, Mrs. Shortridge?"

"Why yes, I believe we do." Mrs. Shortridge was puzzled. "Why do you ask?"

"I'd rather not explain at the moment. I wonder if you could show me the issue which was delivered Tuesday."

Mrs. Shortridge crossed the room to a carved walnut side-table. "I think this is the latest issue."

Joe took the magazine, turned it to read the address label, which, to facilitate post office handling, had been affixed upside down. All seemed in order. "Thank you very much, Mrs. Shortridge. Is Marsh at home?"

"I'll call him." Mrs. Shortridge left the room. Joe looked here and there, studying the fine old furniture, the oriental rugs, the pictures on the walls, the antique clock on the fireplace mantel, the shelves with carefully arranged books. Marsh Shortridge came into the room: a young man with a round, rather flat face, a small nose, a small mouth, eyes which were round and set apart. His hair was soft chestnut, his expression was similar to that of his mother. "Yes, Sheriff."

"I'd like to discuss Ken Mooney with you, Mr. Shortridge."

"I'm afraid I can't help you very much there."

"Maybe yes, maybe no. In a murder investigation we've got to scratch into all sorts of unlikely corners for information and you're one of them."

Marsh's eyebrows took on a quizzical arch. "I'll certainly help you all I can."

"How well did you know Ken?"

"Well enough to say hello to. I had not seen anything of him since high school."

"You know that Bill Whipple was one of Ken's friends?"

Marsh's shrug conveyed ineffable disdain. "Bill Whipple, Ken Mooney…" He said no more.

"Is Bill Whipple one of your good friends?"

"No."

"I see…Well, have you any theory or even a wild guess in relation to the murder?"

"I suppose it must have been the work of a homicidal maniac. I understand that no mail was taken."

"The theory is conceivable, of course. But it doesn't ring true. After Ken was killed the van was hidden all day, then driven down to the end of Madrone Way during the night. This suggests the van was hidden somewhere along Madrone Way — which also means that someone along Madrone Way is the killer."

Marsh smiled his cool little smile. "Most of the people along Madrone are good citizens, Sheriff — solid, conservative folk. One or two exceptions, of course. But I can't imagine anyone along Madrone Way killing Ken Mooney — not for any reason."

"Suppose something came in the mail which would ruin someone's life — suppose a package burst open and spilled an ounce or two of heroin. Suppose somebody received an incriminating postcard which Ken read."

Marsh thought carefully a moment. Then he asked: "Isn't all this pretty hypothetical?"

Joe gave Marsh a look of surprise. "Of course it's hypothetical. What else? I don't have any facts. I'm trying to scare some up."

Marsh shrugged. "I'll certainly help all I can."

"You saw Ken Tuesday morning, I believe."

"He brought me a C.O.D. package. Some books. I paid him, and that was all there was to it."

"How much was the C.O.D.?"

"Ten dollars and sixty-seven cents." Marsh frowned. "Something peculiar there, come to think of it. I started to write him a check and he asked for cash. I told him I didn't have that much on me. He said to write a check for ten dollars and give him sixty-seven cents, which I did."

Joe reflected. "Deardorf took charge of all the C.O.D.s and registered mail. He didn't make any complaint so I guess everything came out even. Well, it may or may not mean anything. Is your sister in the house?"

"I'll call her," said Marsh with alacrity. He departed and presently Starr looked into the room. She wore black slacks, a gray jersey blouse, sandals. She sauntered forward. "I don't know who killed Ken Mooney," she told Joe. "I knew him by sight, not to talk to. Nobody has ever expressed hatred for Ken Mooney in my hearing. I don't know whether or not Ken Mooney was having a love affair with — well, with anybody."

"Did you hear gossip?" asked Joe.

"No."

"Sit down," said Joe. "Dancing from one foot to the other like that makes me nervous."

Starr opened her mouth to retort, then, smiling crookedly, sat down on the couch.

"Let's get back to the gossip," said Joe. "Somebody killed Ken Mooney. Whether or not you knew or liked him is immaterial. He was murdered and the murderer may kill somebody else if he isn't caught. Maybe the gossip will help catch him."

"What I was about to say could not even be dignified by the word 'gossip'. It was no more than a sarcastic remark."

"Let's hear it. I want to know the kind of people I'm dealing with."

"It's quite trivial — something Alice Benjamin told me, as a joke. Her mother doesn't like Mrs. Wagner, who is, well, not discriminating and sometimes — spontaneous. Mrs. Benjamin is very proper. She thought that Mrs. Wagner was over-familiar with Ken. So there it is. The gossip."

"I see. Any more gossip about Ken?"

"Just what I remember from high school. He had the reputation of being a girl chaser, and not too choosy."

Joe nodded. "How well do you know the people along Madrone Way?"

"Not too well." Starr was instantly distant.

"Alice Benjamin?"

"An exception."

"Bill Whipple?"

"Not well."

"Marsh is engaged to Alice, so I understand."

Starr's mouth twitched. "Yes."

"When is the wedding?"

"In the fall."

Joe received the impression that Starr did not care to discuss the subject. "Who do you think killed Ken Mooney?"

Starr shrugged. "I could say Bill Whipple, if only because they knew each other — but it's such a poor reason for suspicion that I wouldn't seriously mention his name."

"Did you ever go out with Ken?"

Starr looked at him with a blank face, her outrage and disgust too vehement to be expressed in words. Finally she said, "No. If that's all you want to ask…"

Joe took his departure, walked slowly down the driveway. He noticed Manuel, the handyman and gardener, and inquired if on Tuesday afternoon the mail van had been parked anywhere on the Shortridge property.

Manuel shook his head, slowly, emphatically. "No place to park any mail van."

"What about under the trees, or behind a bush, or something like that?"

Manuel shrugged. "You show me where."

Joe looked up and down the driveway. "I thought you might know."

Manuel wordlessly resumed his work.

Joe went back to Madrone Way. Opposite was the golf course. People playing golf might have noticed some significant fact. Another job for Rex Kelly, or maybe Fay Insley.

2

Joe walked around the curve of Madrone Way, with the stone wall enclosing the Shortridge property on his left. The stone wall angled up Spanish Hill; a smooth green lawn sloped down to the sidewalk. At the back of the lawn stood a white stucco house with a red tile roof.

Joe walked up the driveway, rang the bell. Mrs. Betty Taylor, a freckle-faced red-haired woman, answered the bell. In the tiled foyer behind her Joe could see two bicycles, a tricycle, three baseball gloves, a bat.

"Yes, sir?" Mrs. Taylor's voice was as bright and cheerful as her appearance.

"I'm Sheriff Joe Bain, Mrs. Taylor; may I come in?"

"If you'll take the risk of picking your way through the mess. I haven't got around to cleaning house."

"I've seen worse," said Joe.

Mrs. Taylor took him into a living room which was furnished more for service than for display. Joe seated himself in a canvas chair while Mrs. Taylor perched on the arm of the sofa. "I suppose you know why I'm here."

Mrs. Taylor's face became alarmed. "What have they done now?"

"In regard to the murder of Ken Mooney."

Mrs. Taylor relaxed. "I know my young devils so well that nothing would surprise me. The way you looked I thought, 'Oh my, this time they've really done something terrible!'"

"Nothing I know of," said Joe. "Were you home Tuesday morning?"

"Yes. My husband was at work; he's with Valley Savings and Loan, as I suppose you know. I can hardly wait till school starts again. My children aren't really bad; they're just boys, and there's always something to send me flying around with my hair on end."

"Did you know Ken Mooney to speak to?"

"Not really. I know what he looked like, and he seemed a pleasant young man."

"Did you see anything Tuesday morning which was at all out of the ordinary?"

"With my four boys, Sheriff, I never see anything else. But aside from the usual cyclone, I didn't see or hear a thing."

"Your husband was at work, of course. What about your boys? How old are they?"

"There's Jeffery 10, Miles 8, Peter 6 and Craig 3. Craig is just starting to run with the others and that means I have to run too. Although I must say that Jeff and Miles are very responsible. Peter is a little stinker when it comes to Craig; he senses competition."

Joe asked, "Did they see anything out of the ordinary on Tuesday?"

"I don't think so. They were business operatives Tuesday with a lemonade stand. I believe they said that the man who was killed owed them a dime and now they'll never collect; heartless little brutes. That's all they could think of: not poor Mr. Mooney or how terrible his wife must feel, but where was their dime?"

"They're just acquiring the business point of view," said Joe. "Maybe I'd better talk to them. Are they anywhere nearby?"

"I think they're out in back building something..."

Jeff and Miles were summoned: sturdy auburn-haired boys in T-shirts and blue jeans. "This is Sheriff Bain, boys. He wants to ask you some questions; please listen carefully and tell him exactly what happened."

"You mean about the guy that got killed?"

"Just answer Sheriff Bain's questions."

"I understand," said Joe, "that Ken Mooney died in debt."

The boys looked at Joe, frowning and doubtful. Jeff, the oldest, said, "He owed us a dime."

The story reached Joe as a rhetorical contest between Jeff and Miles, refereed by Mrs. Taylor. On Tuesday morning they had set up a lemonade stand on Madrone Way opposite the country club entrance. On entering Madrone Way Ken halted the van to rearrange his deliveries and Jeff had shouted a solicitation across the street. After some banter Ken agreed to purchase a glass of lemonade on credit. He had, so he stated, only a ten dollar bill in his possession; he had however a collection to make along Madrone Way and would pay them on his way out. Here Jeff, who was telling the tale, paused for dramatic effect. Miles started to insert the denouement, but Jeffery turned on him and shouted: "Who's telling this story, you or me?"

"Now, boys, don't quarrel," commanded Mrs. Taylor. "Jeffery, you had a turn; let Miles tell part of the story too."

Joe looked at Miles. "He didn't pay you when he came out?"

"He didn't come out!" yelled Jeffery.

"You told my part," bellowed Miles.

"Jeffery, that wasn't very nice," said Mrs. Taylor. "How would you like it if Miles did that to you?"

"He does things like that all day!"

"Just a minute," said Joe. "Let me get a word in edgewise. You say Ken Mooney never came out of Madrone Way? Or the van never came out? Or both?"

"Neither Ken Mooney nor the van came out!"

"Are you sure of this?"

"Of course we're sure! He owed us a dime!"

"How long did you keep your stand open?"

"Until four thirty. That's when we're allowed to look at TV."

"What about lunch time? Did you go in for lunch?"

"And leave our lemonade for people to steal? Huh!"

"I took them some sandwiches and milk," Mrs. Taylor explained. "I thought that they needed a little encouragement."

"They were all peanut butter sandwiches," said Miles with a grimace of distaste. "I like tuna-fish better. Or hamburgers. Oh boy!"

"You're a pair of spoiled brats," said Mrs. Taylor. "Do you know what the children in India have to eat? Just a little bit of rice every day!"

"I like rice," said Jeffery.

"What else did you see, boys?" Joe asked.

"Nothing. We couldn't look around the corner up Madrone Way. He must have got killed just after he left us!"

"Yes, I expect so. Was there anybody in the cab with him?"

"Nope."

"Did he seem worried or excited?"

"Nope. Just like he always was. Kind of laughing and joking."

Joe learned no more. But now it was definite. Ken had been killed by someone along Madrone Way. Somewhere along Madrone Way the van had been concealed, then, during the night, driven to the far end of Madrone Way and abandoned.

Another item of interest: Joe now knew why Ken had insisted on sixty-seven cents cash from Marsh Shortridge — that he might pay his ten-cent debt. So far, so good.

He started to leave, then turned back. "Do you subscribe to *Life* magazine, Mrs. Taylor?"

"Why yes, we do. It's entertaining and occasionally educational."

"May I see the latest copy you received, please? The one that came Tuesday?"

Mrs. Taylor gave him a mystified glance. "Jeffery, run into the family room and bring out the new *Life*. It's right next to your father's desk."

"I'll get it," said Miles.

"No, you won't," said Jeffery, and shoving his brother aside he ran from the room, presently to return with the magazine.

Joe turned it upside down, glanced at the label, leafed casually through the pages, handed it back. "Thank you very much, Mrs. Taylor."

3

The Benjamins lived in a neat gray and white colonial-style house surrounded by immaculate gardens. Mrs. Benjamin, wearing a pale blue maternity dress, a navy blue cardigan and white gloves, stood sprinkling a recently reseeded section of lawn. She was a tall woman, with strongly marked features and gray-blonde hair she did not deign to tint. Joe, no expert in such matters, judged her to be six or seven months along with child. Mrs. Benjamin glanced at him briefly, then returned her attention to the sprinkler. So this prickly-looking specimen had mothered the beautiful Alice. Possibly in her youth Grace Benjamin had also been beautiful, thought Joe, in a cool Easter-lily fashion.

"Mrs. Benjamin?" he asked in his most silken voice.

Only now did Grace Benjamin acknowledge his presence. "Yes?"

"I'm Sheriff Joe Bain. I'd like to ask a few questions."

"In regard to what?"

"The death of Ken Mooney."

Mrs. Benjamin considered, and for a moment Joe thought she was about to say no. She turned off the water, glanced at her wrist watch. "I have a doctor's appointment very shortly; but I can give you a few minutes."

"Thank you, Mrs. Benjamin." Joe looked significantly toward the house but Mrs. Benjamin apparently did not intend to ask him inside. "Well then, did you see Ken Mooney Tuesday morning?"

"No. I was in the back garden. He put the mail in the box and went on by. I don't believe I even noticed the van."

"I see. In a murder investigation, Mrs. Benjamin, I'm forced to ask questions which in other circumstances might be thought impertinent.

So I apologize in advance. By the way, do you have any theories of your own?"

"I had supposed it was a thief, or something of the sort."

"The evidence points in another direction. I understand that your daughter Alice knew Ken at high school."

"She was acquainted with him; yes."

"Did she ever go out with Ken on a date?"

Mrs. Benjamin turned him a cold glance. "No. She did not."

"Alice never mentioned him?"

"I don't believe she ever did."

"Something rather puzzling: Ken had a registered letter for you Tuesday and never delivered it. Have you any idea why that should be?"

Grace Benjamin considered. "Perhaps because I was in the back yard and didn't hear the bell. Usually it sounds loud enough. Or the mailman might have been in a hurry. I suggest you ask Mrs. Wagner next door; she knows him better than I do." And Mrs. Benjamin gave a small sniff.

"Mrs. Wagner was friendly with Ken?"

"Perhaps you had better ask Mrs. Wagner."

Joe forced a laugh. "That's not the theory of interrogation, Mrs. Benjamin. I'm here to gather facts which eventually will help me make an arrest. Just as a wild speculation, suppose that Mrs. Wagner were guilty. She would hardly give me information leading to her own downfall. I have to get the incriminating facts from her friends and neighbors."

Grace Benjamin smiled a brief prim smile. "Mrs. Wagner has her peculiarities but to suspect her of murder is ridiculous. And I really don't care to gossip."

"I don't want gossip, I want facts. How well acquainted, from your personal knowledge, were Mrs. Wagner and Ken Mooney?"

"She occasionally invited him in for a cup of coffee or a dish of ice cream."

"How do you know this?"

Grace Benjamin smiled once again. "Mrs. Wagner has a loud voice. If she asks, 'cream and sugar?' I suppose she's serving coffee. If she asks 'chocolate syrup or plain?' I presume she's serving ice cream."

"Hm, ahem. Did she ever, in your hearing, give Ken his choice of anything else?"

"Not in my hearing."

"I understand your daughter is marrying Marsh Shortridge."

"Yes, in September."

"When is she returning from Europe?"

"Toward the end of August. Mr. Benjamin invited the two of them to India for a honeymoon, but Marshall for some reason decided against this. I gave her a summer in Europe instead. It's the last freedom she'll be having." Joe was somewhat surprised by the cynicism in Mrs. Benjamin's voice. Quickly she went on to say, "The Shortridges of course are a wonderful family and Marshall is an excellent match. I am very pleased for her."

"Is Mr. Benjamin returning for the wedding?"

"I hardly think so. But how does all this concern the dead mailman?"

"Probably not at all," said Joe. "I'm just groping."

Mrs. Benjamin glanced at her watch.

"One last thing," said Joe. "Do you subscribe to *Life* magazine?"

"Yes." Mrs. Benjamin turned him a cool glance. "What of it?"

"May I see the current issue?"

Mrs. Benjamin frowned, started to speak, then shrugged and turned away. "It's in the house. Do you care to come in?"

"If it's more convenient for you."

Mrs. Benjamin walked slowly up the steps. She opened the door; they went into the house. It was evident that Mrs. Benjamin was a meticulous housekeeper. The furniture glowed with wax; silver glistened; the carpets appeared freshly brushed and vacuumed. On the grand piano, in a silver frame, was a photograph of Alice; apparently a high school graduation picture. "This must be your daughter," said Joe.

"Yes."

"I believe I've seen her around town. My daughter knew her at high school."

"Really… Here is the magazine."

Joe glanced at the now-familiar cover, read the label, and as before pretended to look through the pages. Mrs. Benjamin watched with detached curiosity. "May I ask what you are looking for?"

"You could ask, Mrs. Benjamin, but for now I'd prefer not to tell you. It's just a little idea of mine."

"I see. I'm in just a bit of a hurry, so if you'll excuse me..."

"Certainly. Thank you for your help."

4

Sally Wagner lived in the most modern house on Madrone Way: an informal single-storied cottage with rustic redwood siding and picture windows offering views of everything nearby, including the fence which concealed all but the second-story bedroom windows of the Benjamin residence next door. Sally Wagner herself was a shrewd vivacious woman of thirty-five or so: garrulous, affable, bumptious, without tact or reserve. Her least attractive feature was her voice. She spoke in a nasal caw as if her sinuses were congested. She wore her black hair in bangs; her eyes looked forth from puddles of blue-green eye shadow; she wore a scarlet jacket, black stretch pants, white sandals. All in all, thought Joe, just the woman to arouse Grace Benjamin's most emphatic disapproval.

Sally Wagner said as much herself. "If you've been talking to Mrs. Benjamin you've probably heard an earful in regard to me. She figures me a sure bet for the Hot Place. I smoke, I drink, I hold hands, I kick up my heels — in short I don't care a damn."

"Mrs. Benjamin didn't put it in quite those words," said Joe tactfully.

"I expect she wouldn't," declared Sally Wagner in scorn. "She'd hint and shake her head and sniff. Poor Guy Benjamin! He takes those long foreign contracts to avoid staying at home. I'm surprised he got her pregnant. He was home during the Christmas holidays; the time works out right: don't worry, I've counted."

Joe grinned, leaned back in the chair. In spite of her glottal voice Sally Wagner agreeably counteracted the chill of the Benjamin house. "Let me open you a can of beer," she offered. "It must be hot work talking to a pack of females."

"Well, let's see. I've talked to one, two, three, four, five females, counting you, one male and two boys. Mostly females, I'll agree."

"What did you learn, if anything?"

"I know for sure Ken was killed along Madrone Way. Did you mention beer? I shouldn't be mooching from you, but you're right, I'm dying of thirst."

Sally Wagner trotted into her kitchen, returned pouring beer into a tall glass. "There. That looks so good I think I'll have one myself." A moment later she returned. "Now. I suppose you want to ask if I killed Ken Mooney. No, I did not. Poor Ken. Such a lamb, so nice, so innocent. Not much ambition, but if everybody was admiral, who'd row the boat?"

"You knew Ken pretty well then?"

Sally Wagner's black eyes snapped, whether in amusement or vexation Joe could not be sure. "I want to tell you one thing — any filthy innuendos from next door are just that. Ken reminded me of how things used to be. It was pleasant to hear him talk. I'd sometimes ask him in for a cup of coffee; sometimes he'd come, sometimes not."

"What about Tuesday?"

"I didn't see him at all. He just pushed my mail in the box and hurried off."

"What's your idea about the murder?"

"Quite frankly, Sheriff, I'm bewildered. It all seems utterly pointless and foolish. It seems — unreal!"

"He never mentioned enemies?"

"He hardly knew what the word meant. On the other hand he had no close friends. He knew Bill Whipple down the street of course. His home life must have been ghastly. You should hear the tales of his father's economies. A regular miser! I suppose you know that Ken came from a very old local family?"

"Yes, so I heard. Incidentally, while I think of it, do you subscribe to *Life*?"

"No! I certainly do not!" With great animation Sally Wagner explained her opinion of Henry Luce. "Why do you ask?"

"Something has come up in the course of the investigation."

Sally Wagner danced up and down like a small girl. "I bet I know! Wasn't there a magazine under Ken's head?"

"Yes, as a matter of fact. Where did you hear that?"

"From Laura Hubman. She heard all the gory details from her mother's nurse, the one who found the body."

"Well, that's the reason for my interest. What do you know of the Whipples next door?"

"I see very little of them. Sheila Whipple is just a bit pushy. I'm sure she pushed Fred Whipple into moving out here on Madrone. He's an ordinary sort, a hard worker, spends a lot of time hunting and fishing. Neither of them makes any intellectual pretensions. *There* you'll probably find a *Life* subscription, and *Reader's Digest* and *Playboy*. As for Bill..." Sally Wagner pouted thoughtfully. "Well, I don't know. He's a complicated young man. He can be extremely charming when he wants to be. College has taken off some of his rough edges — but sharpened up some of the others. He's got a terrible reputation girl-wise, of course."

Joe spent another half hour listening to Sally Wagner's plangent voice; then, thanking her for the beer, he took his leave.

5

Joe pressed the Whipple doorbell. Once. Twice. Three times. No one responded.

He walked past the home of Milo Gentry, the oldest of the County Supervisors. Milo and Ernestine Gentry were visiting their grandchildren in Montana.

In the house beyond lived Mr. and Mrs. Caspar Hubman. Laura Hubman opened the door, a woman about forty-five, of lavish and spectacular appearance. She was tall, ample of bosom and hip, willowy and youthful through the waist. Her skin was marmoreal, her hair black and flowing; and in spite of her emphatic vitality, she was pleased to demonstrate the languid manner of a pre-Raphaelite poetess. She wore an extravagant black satin tea gown which swept the floor, black ballet slippers, a single ivory disk dangling from her right ear.

Joe introduced himself. "I'm Sheriff Joe Bain. I believe we've met before, somewhere or other."

"Perhaps at a school function," said Mrs. Hubman. "Caspar and I are active politically, of course." She had an easy husky voice. "Well, you're probably here to ask about Ken Mooney."

"Yes. I'm afraid that's the case."

"Please come in." Laura Hubman took him into a carefully bizarre living room. She seated him on an extremely low Korean couch, while she herself perched on a five-foot stool, so that Joe was forced to look up at her from between his knees.

"Caspar is writing," said Laura Hubman. "I can call him if you like."

"No, I'd just as soon talk with you."

Laura Hubman laughed. "He's a better conversationalist, but he tends to become didactic. Well then, what do you want to know?"

"Well, if you killed Ken Mooney, I wish you'd confess and save us all time and worry."

"I'm sorry, Sheriff."

Joe picked up a copy of *Réalités* from an exquisite ebony tabouret inlaid with mother-of-pearl. "By any chance, do you subscribe to *Life* magazine?"

"Heavens no." Laura Hubman swayed on the tall stool as if in shock.

"Did you speak to Ken Tuesday morning?"

"No. I was potting — doing ceramics, you know — in my studio. Caspar was in his study working on his book. When we came up for air, the mail was in the box. So really we can't tell you a thing."

"You knew Ken?"

"Not really. I've had occasion to speak to him. He'd go into my mother's house and drink her wine, and then she'd drink, and it was so bad for her, because the doctor specifically warned her against alcohol and any kind of excitement." Laura Hubman's voice briefly took on animation. "But that's neither here nor there. I simply asked Ken not to excite Mama, and he said he wouldn't. Caspar of course knew him at high school."

Caspar Hubman peered into the room, then entered: a portly gentleman about his wife's age. He was almost bald; he wore horn-rim spectacles, a pair of maroon shorts and a yellow terry-cloth polo shirt. Caspar Hubman was bellwether for the intellectuals of Pleasant Grove — a somewhat sparse contingent, to be sure — and he was writing a book. Joe had encountered Caspar Hubman on several other occasions and tended to find him perplexing. Still, he conducted the high school with reasonable efficiency and seemed to be well liked by the students.

"Well, Sheriff, no mystery why you're here," said Hubman. "Do you have any notion as to what happened?"

"I was about to ask you the same question."

Hubman gave a perfunctory chuckle. "I can't give you any help. I wish I could. Ken was a fine young man."

"Did you see him Tuesday morning?"

"No. I saw the van pull up by the mailbox, but paid no great attention."

"Any theory why anyone would want to kill Ken?"

"Not one in the world. At school he was popular with everyone."

Joe considered his next question. Laura sat watching intently. Caspar stood thumbs in waistband drumming his paunch. Laura suddenly jumped down from the stool. Joe wondered if she were nervous and, if so, why. He asked, "Did Ken ever mention any of his personal business? Ever talk about his girl friends or anything of the sort?"

"Never," said Laura. Too quickly? Too sharply?

"He'd have no reason to," declared Caspar.

Joe's legs began to cramp. He stood up, looked for some place to sit. There was the five-foot stool, the Korean couch, some modern furniture he wasn't sure how to get into. He remained standing. On a table, among other magazines, he noticed a *Life*. He picked it up, turned it over to read the address label. Laura Hubman said quickly, "My mother subscribes to a lot of magazines. Sometimes she passes them on to us."

Joe asked every question which seemed relevant, a few which did not. Caspar and Laura responded warily, always as if searching the questions for ambiguity. Not necessarily a sign of guilt, reflected Joe. Few people remained at ease during police interrogation, especially when the subject of the conversation was murder.

Finally, with Caspar sweating and fidgeting and Laura clenching and unclenching her fists, Joe took his leave. "If you think of anything I forgot to ask about, please let me know."

"We surely will," declared Caspar Hubman.

6

The Wilfred Mortimer house was empty. Joe walked up the driveway, inspected the premises. As Rex Kelly had averred, there was no sign of burglary or extraordinary activity. The garage was locked; nowhere else could the van have been concealed. Joe stood a moment thinking.

The systematics of the murder were becoming somewhat clearer — or, at least, the areas of ignorance were contracting. The testimony of Jeff and Miles Taylor certified that Ken had been killed somewhere along Madrone Way, at a time after he had delivered the Mortimer mail. The scene of the crime would then seem to be near at hand: the Mortimer driveway? What then? In theory the van could have been driven off the Shortridge driveway and hidden behind shrubbery, but only a madman would have dared the attempt. The Taylor driveway? Not a chance, with Jeffery, Miles, Peter and Craig roving the premises. In addition, there was only a car-port, no garage. Mrs. Benjamin had a neat garage which might well have hidden the van, as did Sally Wagner, the Whipples, the Hubmans and Mrs. Bazzarini. The Gentry garage was locked, so was the Mortimers'.

Joe walked back to inspect the Gentry driveway, which was bordered by beds of petunia, dusty miller and snapdragon. Emphatically the van had not been driven across these beds. The lock on the Gentry garage was intact. Was it possible that Mrs. Cream, the colored housekeeper, were murderess or accomplice? Joe peered intently at the spider web which connected the garage door to the soffit above. Practical detection! The spider web was more than two days old, by the evidence of several desiccated flies. Mrs. Cream was no longer a suspect.

Returning to the Mortimer house, Joe scrutinized the garage door hoping to find another spider web. None could be seen. The wind, however, had blown leaves across the driveway and Joe decided that no post office van had been driven across them.

He now proceeded to Mrs. Bazzarini's house: an enormous three-story structure with brown shingle siding. The Bazzarini garage was closest to the spot where the van had been discovered. In fact, if given a slight initial push, a vehicle might have rolled from the garage out upon Madrone Way.

Joe turned up toward the house. The curtains at the window quivered and fell back. Mrs. Bazzarini kept a close watch on the events of Madrone Way.

Miss Locke, who had discovered Ken's body, answered the doorbell. She made cryptic gestures toward the sitting room, which Joe understood as an injunction against excitement, then ushered Joe into the front room. Mrs. Bazzarini was a white-haired woman of average size, not obviously ill. In her eyes and nose and the carriage of her head Joe saw a resemblance to her daughter Laura, and there was even a bit of Laura Hubman's vitality in Mrs. Bazzarini's attentiveness. "I'm back again, Mrs. Bazzarini. I've got a few more questions in regard to Ken Mooney."

"Who did it?" demanded Mrs. Bazzarini. "I want him sent to the electric chair. He killed a real nice boy, who was so kind and good." She shook her head, blew her long nose in a paper handkerchief.

"I'll find the guilty person, don't worry about that," said Joe. "But I want your help."

"You can count on me for anything. Why did they have to harm a nice boy like Ken? So many no-good bums in the world and they pick on Ken! He always had a nice word for me, a sick old lady. If he had time he'd come in and talk. I get so lonesome! He was really full of kindness and goodness — more than my own flesh and blood, I admit it!"

"He spent quite a bit of time here?" asked Joe.

"Depending on how much work he had. If he was late he sometimes came in and ate his lunch, and I always had a glass of wine for him. Usually he came earlier, at ten or eleven."

"You knew him pretty well then."

"I should say so. He told me all about his family — his father was a hard stubborn man, Sheriff. He told me about his place in the mountains and what he wanted to make with it."

"What about his girl friends?"

"He never talked much about girls. He was a sensible boy, though you'd never think so till you knew him. I just can't understand who would want to hit him like that! It must have been a crazy man! Or maybe it was something connected with the mail."

Joe nodded soberly. "Quite possibly true. But why didn't Ken deliver your mail on Tuesday? He delivered the Mortimer house, and that's all until we find him dead the next morning."

"Well — it wasn't Ken, you know," said Mrs. Bazzarini doubtfully.

"What?"

"I just glimpsed him go up the Mortimer driveway, and it wasn't Ken. I guess it was the substitute carrier."

"Is that so? What did he look like?"

"I couldn't tell you. He didn't walk like Ken. He was in a hurry, almost running. Ken used to amble, just slouch along."

"Was he big? little? fat? thin?"

"Just about medium-sized, I'd say. But I couldn't really swear to anything. I just had a little glimpse."

"Well, well, well." Joe rubbed his forehead. "Are you sure of this?"

"It's what I thought. I used to watch for Ken, and I was disappointed when he didn't come. I thought maybe he was sick or something like that."

"Incidentally," said Joe, "I understand that you subscribe to *Life*."

"Yes, I like to read, and keep up with things."

"Where is the new magazine?"

"Why, I don't know. I've been so upset, I don't believe I've seen it. Barbara!" Mrs. Bazzarini called Miss Locke. "Did you see the new *Life* anywhere?"

Miss Locke looked rather vaguely around the room. "I don't see it, Mrs. Bazzarini."

"Don't worry. I can do without."

"Selma might have taken it over to your daughter's. She took over a big armful of magazines yesterday."

The idea of Caspar and Laura receiving Mrs. Bazzarini's old magazines struck Joe as rather ludicrous. "Is Mrs. Hubman your only child, Mrs. Bazzarini?"

"Yes. I once had a boy, but he got killed in an auto accident. A long time ago. Maybe that's why I was so fond of Ken. He reminded me of Raymond. I gave Laura her house, I've given them money, I sent them on a fine trip to Europe, and they never come to see me, even though they live so close. They just let me sit here and be sick, but Ken would always have time to say a nice word or two. Don't worry, I had him down for something in my will. I wasn't going to forget him." Mrs. Bazzarini's face began to quiver. "I don't know what I'm going to do."

Miss Locke made a significant gesture to Joe, who hastily withdrew.

7

Joe stood at the end of Madrone Way where the mail van had been found. Things were more confused than ever. Ken Mooney had driven his van into Madrone Way, he had bought a glass of lemonade on cred-it, he had delivered a C.O.D. package to Marsh Shortridge. Sometime later Mrs. Bazzarini claimed to have seen a mailman, not Ken Mooney, delivering mail to the Mortimer house.

A car pulled up to the curb; Howard Griselda, owner and editor of the *Pleasant Grove Messenger*, alighted.

Joe managed a limp gesture of greeting. "Hello, Howard."

Griselda nodded. "What does it look like, Sheriff?"

"A mess. That's not for publication. I can't decide what's going on. That's also not for publication."

"What is for publication then?" asked Griselda, carefully loading his pipe.

"Just the bare facts. Ken Mooney came into Madrone Way. He never left. Somehow he got lured into turning off the street and was killed. That's all I know for sure. It looks as if the murderer must live along Madrone Way, on account of the logistics of the crime. I mean by this that the van was parked somewhere all day, probably in somebody's garage, then brought out late at night and abandoned, but not too far away from the murderer's home."

Howard Griselda gave a series of pontifical nods. "That seems straightforward enough. How do you know Ken never left Madrone Way?"

Joe reported the evidence of Jeff and Miles Taylor, with Griselda nodding and puffing on his pipe.

"Isn't it all very simple then?" asked Griselda. "Just find where the deliveries stopped and you've got your killer."

Joe shook his head. "The last delivery was to an empty house. And Mrs. Bazzarini didn't kill Ken for about nine reasons. First of all, she was fond of him. Second, she's in a wheel chair and has just about strength enough to whack a cat with a teaspoon. Third, her nurses would forbid her to strain herself. Fourth, she's the most unreasonable prospect on the block, with the exception of Mrs. Cream. I'd suspect you first, Howard."

Griselda acknowledged the witticism with a saturnine smile. "Seems to me the basic question here is: did the murderer kill Ken Mooney, or did he kill the postman?"

"That's what I'm working on." Joe looked off down Madrone Way. "Which means I've got to intrude into the private lives of everyone along this street, and they're all going to be vexed."

Griselda shrugged. "You wanted the job. All you have to do now is cut the mustard."

"I'll promise you one thing, Howard. Whenever I feel like resigning, you'll be the first to hear about it."

Howard Griselda placidly puffed on his pipe. "Incidentally, Sheriff, I hear of strange goings-on at the jail, in connection with a prisoner named Juan Carminez."

"Oh, ah," said Joe.

"Yep. Seems as if Carminez stepped out to visit his boy at the hospital." He eyed Joe quizzically. Joe looked across the golf course. "I checked at the hospital and it seems that the boy came in with a burst appendix and in a state of acute depression. Some people by the name of Aguilar had been taunting him with the fact that his father was in jail. Well, to make a long story short, Dr. Berry tells me that Carminez' visit to the hospital probably saved the boy's life. Carminez subsequently went out and assaulted Aguilar." He paused, looked inquiringly at Joe, who gave a curt nod.

"So I was told."

"That story is news," said Griselda. "I'd like to run it. What if Carminez had stabbed Aguilar as he stabbed Henry Gutierrez? You'd be in a rough position, Sheriff."

"Possibly so, Howard."

"The fact remains, I can't print the story because the public would ignore the impropriety and think only of the boy's troubles. You'll get by with this one."

"I wasn't worried, Howard. Where did you get the information?"

"Sources, Sheriff, sources."

"I know you'd like to prove me a crook, Howard; I'm afraid you're in for a hard pull."

"I don't want to prove you a crook. I just feel that temperamentally you're not the man for the job. San Rodrigo County isn't the backwoods. It's a thriving progressive county in the center of California. We want an up-to-date progressive law-enforcement system, not a sheriff's office which casually turns loose prisoners and then forgets about them."

"Well, I could use more deputies and a full-time booking sergeant. Also I'm miserably underpaid: about the lowest salary in the state. If you want a big-time production, get me some big-time money."

"You'll have to take that up with the voters."

Joe laughed. "The trouble is, we've got a low crime rate, due to the efficiency of the sheriff's office. People don't want to put out money to see me ride a white horse in the July Fourth parade, like old Cooch used to do. Where he got the money I won't even guess."

Chapter VII

1

IN THE SOUREST OF MOODS Joe went home for lunch. Miranda was visiting a friend; his mother, after several attempts to make conversation, became offended and went off into the living room to watch television. Joe ate cold ham and potato salad in solitude. Now he had two mysteries on his hands: who killed Ken Mooney and who tipped off Howard Griselda in regard to Juan Carminez?

In the latter case Miss Curdy was not automatically to blame. Conceivably the Aguilars had been sufficiently astounded by the miracle of one Juan Carminez locked up in jail and another identical Juan Carminez performing an assault at La Fiesta to report the case to Howard Griselda.

Joe snapped open a can of beer. Forget Juan Carminez and the Aguilars! Who had killed Ken Mooney?

There was, of course, the question Howard Griselda had propounded: had the murder been done to Ken Mooney or to the postman?

Joe went to the telephone, called Henry Deardorf, the postmaster. "Sheriff Joe Bain here, Postmaster. In regard to the Mooney case, do you have anything new?"

"Not a thing." Deardorf's voice was cool.

"I'm wondering if there might have been some kind of mail delivered along Madrone Way that was, well, outrageous or scandalous."

Deardorf stated that the mail delivered along Madrone Way and all throughout Pleasant Grove was so inoffensive as to be insipid.

"Is there some kind of mail that people might feel guilty about receiving?"

Deardorf spoke with patient reasonableness: "If they kill the post office employees they will not receive this mail, so they are defeating their own purposes."

"I was thinking about mail someone hadn't been expecting — a post card from a girl friend, or say a fan letter from Fidel, something of the sort."

"Anything's possible," said Deardorf, "but if you think we sit around the post office drinking hot chocolate and reading post cards you're wrong."

"No offense meant, Mr. Deardorf. I'm just trying to get to the bottom of things."

"I wish you would, and pretty quick too. You can't imagine the questions people are asking us."

"I'm making progress, Mr. Deardorf. The first step in an investigation is getting the facts."

The conversation came to an end. Joe telephoned headquarters, and spoke to Miss Curdy. The office seemed to be functioning smoothly. Miss Curdy had two matters to call to Joe's attention: "Burt Rank, Director of the Mosquito Abatement Program, wants you to get in touch with him."

"I'll see to his business this afternoon. Anything else?"

"Mr. Griselda telephoned, inquiring about the Carminez affair." Miss Curdy's voice was flat and passionless.

"Hmm. I wonder how he got wind of that?"

"He didn't say."

"I'm going up to the Mooney place for an hour or two. If anything breaks, have Ace give me a call."

Joe opened another can of beer. The Mooney affair was baffling. There had to be a reason for the murder, but none of the customary motives made sense. Mrs. Benjamin had hinted that Sally Wagner's generosity toward Ken was boundless: maybe so. Would either Mrs. Benjamin or Mrs. Wagner kill Ken on this account?

Far-fetched.

Mrs. Bazzarini also liked Ken. She had been planning to leave him a little something in her will. Would the Hubmans, her presumable heirs, slaughter Ken on this account?

Unlikely.

There were Bill Whipple, Alice Benjamin, Starr Shortridge, Marsh

Shortridge, who had known Ken at high school. Was Ken interfering with the goals of one of these?

Hard to believe.

Still, someone had killed Ken, and presumably for an excellent reason. Joe drained the can of beer, set it down with a rap. More facts. More leg work. First out to the Mooney ranch on Oatfarm Road. The two girls, Ken's sisters, perhaps had known more than they had let on. Someone at the country club might have noticed something. Most of all, Joe wanted to talk to Bill Whipple. He telephoned Whipple Chevrolet, but Bill Whipple was out for the day.

Well, then, to Oatfarm Road, for another session with the Mooneys. There was also the matter of Halfway House. Twenty-five thousand dollars seemed a sensible price. Too bad he couldn't slap a few bundles of hundred-dollar bills down on the table in front of Clarence Mooney. Also, while he was in the vicinity, the matter of 'Luna' and her mosquitos.

2

Joe drove north along the Aurora highway, turned right on Hankinson Road. Just past the Oatfarm Road intersection was the real estate office Joe had noticed before: a quaint little fairy-cottage with concave gables and bull's-eye windows. Overhead hung the sign:

PANDORA REALTY
Homes • Farm Properties • Lots
Ring Bell For Attention, Please

Beyond was a driveway bordered by hollyhocks leading to a neat white house under four giant oak trees.

Joe drove into the driveway. To the east side of the house were twelve shallow concrete pans, six feet by two feet, arranged in a circle like the spokes of a wheel, each containing two inches of water. Joe could understand Burt Rank's anguish.

Joe parked under the oak trees, looked right and left for dogs, stepped out of the car. A pleasant place, with the rolling hills just behind, the valley stretching away into the summer haze.

He went to the door at the front of a screened porch, pressed the button. From a far distance came a tinkle as of wind chimes or delicate glass bells…Joe touched the button a second time. Again the tinkle of bells. He wondered if 'Luna' were home. A blue Dodge station wagon, three or four years old, stood at the end of the driveway.

Hmm, thought Joe. He turned, reached for the doorbell again, to find Luna already out on the porch, staring at him with lustrous eyes.

Joe, not having heard the door open, jerked back. Luna opened the screen door, stepped outside: a woman about thirty years old, tall and slender, with long black hair constrained by a ribbon of woven copper. She wore a long gown of blue gauze, and Joe apologized hurriedly: "I'm sorry, I didn't mean to get you out of bed."

Luna made a reassuring gesture. "These are my summer garments."

"They look cool," said Joe. "You are 'Luna'?"

Luna nodded. "Yes."

"I'm Sheriff Joe Bain. Mr. Rank asked me to stop by. He feels that there's been some misunderstanding about the mosquito abatement program, and he asked me to straighten things out."

"Yes, it's quite true. I tried to make him understand but I'm sure he went away perplexed."

"Perplexed and unhappy," said Joe. "He feels that stagnant water like this breeds mosquitos, which then become a nuisance and a health hazard."

Luna smiled wistfully. "Poor Mr. Rank, he thinks only of mosquitos, which must become tiresome."

"I suspect that it is. Well, what can we do about those pans?"

"Nothing whatever," said Luna with engaging simplicity.

Joe went to look down into the water. "Look! See those things? Wrigglers!"

Luna bent to peer down into the water. She was slender, but by no means gaunt, and she made, Joe thought, a very attractive picture: very graceful, very stimulating.

" 'Wrigglers'?"

"Baby mosquitos, so to speak."

Luna turned a thoughtful glance toward the sky. "I wonder…I haven't been making really good contact."

"How could it be otherwise? If you like I'll help you clear up the infestation."

"Would you really? How?"

"Easy. I'll just tilt up the pans, dump out the water."

Luna expressed concern for the alignment of the pans, but Joe reassured her; and he was able to lift each pan, spill the water and return the pan to its precise position.

Luna examined the dank concrete surfaces. "They need a good scrubbing before I fill them again."

Joe cautiously inquired if perhaps the pans might not work just as well empty.

Luna laughed and shook her head. "Of course not."

"Have you ever tried?" Joe persisted. "You might be surprised."

"No, I've never tried. I just know they wouldn't work that way."

"What about your husband?" asked Joe. "Has he tried?"

"There isn't any such person. Not on Earth…But what have you done to your hand?"

"Just a little scratch. There was a nail sticking out of that last pan."

Luna expressed distress and pity. She certainly seemed a warm-hearted woman, thought Joe.

"Come inside. I'll help you as best I can."

"It's really nothing much."

Luna insisted and took Joe into the house, where she applied iodine and an aromatic ointment.

"Now, please rest. I'll steep a pot of tea."

Joe sat down on a couch while Luna went off into the kitchen. He picked up a magazine, *The Atlantis*, and started to read an article concerning the anti-gravitic properties of a substance called *zoranium*. Luna returned, wheeling the teapot on a little cart and once again Joe noticed her deft grace and the ease of her motions.

Luna poured the tea, which gave off a pungent odor. Joe sipped cautiously, then, jerking back his head, frowned down into the cup. "What on earth is it?"

"An infusion of nutritious herbs. Try one of these little cakes. I bake them from natural seeds and fibers."

Joe tasted one of the cakes. "What kind of seeds do you use? Not morning-glory seeds, I hope. On second thought, don't tell me. Are you acquainted with Howard Griselda?"

"No. Who is he?"

"A fellow I know. He'd love to find me sprawled out on a divan eating hashish."

Luna smilingly sipped her tea. "What a strange person he must be."

"I agree…My word, this tea has a grip. I feel lucky just getting my tongue back."

"I know over a thousand infusions," said Luna. "Each has its uses." She described the formulation of several representative brews. Joe took another tentative sip, thinking that if Luna poured a cup into each of her concrete pans, there would be no further problem with the mosquitos. "Incidentally," he asked, "what do you achieve with those pans of water?"

Luna considered a moment before replying. "Are you acquainted with Transcendentalism?"

"I confess to ignorance," said Joe.

"In that case," said Luna, "it's rather hard to explain. And I'm not even sure I have the correct orientation."

"If you'd put DDT in the water, or kerosene, or even Clorox everybody would be happy, and I imagine they'd focus about as well as before."

Luna agreed that the plan was worth a trial. "Mr. Rank suggested something similar — but he made it sound so absurd. I'm very sensitive to the umbra which surrounds people. Mr. Rank…" Luna shook her head, reluctant to denigrate a person not present.

Joe ran his hand through his hair, looked over his shoulder. "I won't ask about mine. I felt pretty dim when I arrived. That herb tea or whatever it was lit me up. Do you live out here alone?"

"Yes, I was sent from Arthemisia on a mission which has not yet been revealed to me."

"Arthemisia?" Joe reflected. "Where's that?"

"Arthemisia is a far planet," said Luna. "I seldom speak of it. Most people are frightened; when they can't understand, they become hostile."

"This is pretty far out in the country for a nice-looking woman to be living alone," said Joe. "There's all kinds of people on the loose nowadays, as witness the two of us."

"I'm not afraid."

"I wish I could say the same." Joe rose to his feet and went to look at a complicated lute-like instrument. He touched the strings, evoking a sweet twanging sound. "Are you a musician?"

"Not really. I just sing songs of my native planet."

"I probably couldn't make head or tail of them," said Joe, "but I'd still like to hear you sing."

Luna was obviously pleased by Joe's interest. "I'll practice first, so I won't seem an utter idiot."

"Sometime soon," said Joe. "But now, I'd better be on my way. You remember about those mosquitos, so I don't have to listen to any more of Rank's complaints."

"Kerosene, DDT, or Clorox. I'll try to remember."

3

The Mooney ranch at first glance seemed deserted. Sunlight vibrated off the composition shingles of the house; the windmill creaked; Clarence Mooney's old Chevrolet was nowhere in evidence.

Joe got out of the car and stood in the noonday shimmer. A shadow passed behind one of the windows. A moment later the door opened and the older of the two girls looked out.

"Hi," said Joe. "Where's your father?"

"He went into town."

"Is your mother home?"

"No. They went to arrange the funeral. Stella and I are home alone."

"Well, I'd like to talk to you and your sister."

"I'll go get her — unless you'd like to come in. We're mopping the floor."

"Best talk out here, then."

The other girl appeared; the two sat on the steps, clutching cotton skirts around their bony knees. "I don't think I know your names," said Joe. "I'm Sheriff Bain; I guess you know that."

"That's Stella. I'm Ennis."

"Well, girls," said Joe, "as you know I want to find out who killed Ken. Have you any ideas?" He looked from one thin face to the other.

Ennis and Stella, squinting in concentration, shook their heads.

"Did Ken ever mention his girl friends?"

"Once in a while," said Ennis.

"Who was he going with?"

"Nobody special. Somebody called Helen, once in a while. There was another girl he knew in Panoche."

"Did he go out much with Alice Benjamin?"

"Not very much," said Stella.

Ennis frowned, looked sidewise at her sister.

"When was the last time?" asked Joe.

Ennis said in a disparaging voice, "He hardly ever went with her. In fact I don't think he ever took her out."

Stella, the younger and more vivacious, said, "He used to tell us to drink milk and eat ice cream, so we could grow up to look like Alice."

"Did Ken talk much about Bill Whipple?"

"Not too much. Dad doesn't like him very much. He cheated Dad when we bought our car."

"Oh? How so?"

"Bill wouldn't pay Daddy what our old car was worth," piped Stella. "Then the car used lots of gas and oil. It needed spark-plugs and things like that."

"I guess that's a pretty common occurrence," said Joe. "Do your folks know anybody else along Madrone Way?"

"Mom went to school with Mrs. Shortridge," said Stella. "Up in Coyote. It was just a little two-room school called Iron House School. That was when Mom was a little girl. Afterward Mrs. Shortridge moved to Palo Alto."

Ennis pointed. "Mom and Dad are coming."

The gray Chevrolet rumbled into the driveway, coasted to a stop. Clarence Mooney, in a reddish-brown suit, opened the car door, looked out toward Joe and the two girls for a long frowning moment. He turned, muttered something to his wife, then heaved himself from the car.

Joe rose to his feet, took a few steps forward. "I happened to be in the neighborhood, so I thought I'd see if you had any new ideas regarding Ken."

"Yes, I have," said Clarence Mooney. "I think it was a mistake! I think whoever killed Ken got hold of the wrong man!"

"It's a thought," Joe conceded. "So far as I'm concerned, there are three main possibilities, one in connection with Alice Benjamin, one with Bill Whipple, and one with Mrs. Bazzarini."

Clarence Mooney gave a sour grunt. "I don't know Mrs. Bazzarini or the other, but I know Bill Whipple. I wouldn't put much past him. There's a self-centered young fellow for you, Sheriff. He treated Ken like he was a chuckle-head — me too, for that matter. Told me he'd take Halfway House off my hands if I wasn't in any hurry for my money. Can you imagine that?"

"Pretty wild. How much did he offer you?"

"Not enough. He was a bad influence on Ken, if you want my opinion — gave Ken all kinds of wrong ideas."

"Such as how?"

"Well, the easy attitude toward life. Easy money, easy girls. Conniving instead of working. Cheating a man, instead of dealing fair and square and giving him his money's worth. Mind you, I don't mean to say that Ken took to any of this; he didn't, because he wasn't brought up that way. But maybe Ken wavered just a bit. You could see him wondering, and maybe he spent more foolish money than he might have otherwise."

"How did Ken get along with the people he worked with?"

"He never said too much."

Mrs. Mooney interposed timidly: "You remember how Ken didn't like Mr. Deardorf?"

"That wasn't anything," growled Clarence Mooney. "Nothing worthwhile talking about. One day Deardorf found Ken reading magazines from the mail while he was eating his lunch, and gave him a lecture. Ken didn't like it."

"I don't blame him," declared Mrs. Mooney. "What harm was he doing?"

"It's not a matter of harm," said Clarence Mooney. "Rules are rules. If you break one, you go on to break another."

"Something in that," said Joe. "By the way, I just happened to mention to my mother that Halfway House was up for sale. She was mildly interested, provided the price was right. I know she wouldn't go anywhere near forty thousand dollars."

Clarence Mooney listened with a small quiet smile. Joe saw that he was up against a real pro.

"I'd like to be generous," said Mooney regretfully. "If I had millions of dollars I'd give money away. But things are tight. I've had some nibbles at forty-five thousand and I was thinking about accepting. At forty thousand I'm taking a beating. I couldn't undercut that figure very much, if at all."

"Place is about ready to collapse," said Joe. "It needs everything from new pipes to clean bedspreads. I told my mother but she's a sentimental old girl; she remembers the place like it used to be forty years ago."

"Forty years ago Halfway House was famous," stated Clarence Mooney. "Up and down the coast."

"True. But now it's unknown. I put all those facts to my mother but she told me go ahead, make Mr. Mooney an offer."

"An offer, hey? Well, I'll listen. I can always say no. How much?"

"Twenty-four thousand seven hundred. That's taking every cent of her insurance, all her savings, the works."

"If she's got twenty-four thousand there's no problem. She can borrow another fifteen, I mean sixteen, with no trouble at all. She'd be doing herself a favor. A big hotel man from San Francisco would take it right now at forty thousand. I said, 'I want to keep it in local hands.'"

"I hardly think she'll go that high. It's a quaint old ruin, but forty grand is a lot of money."

Clarence Mooney looked at Joe sidewise, with a mixture of mulishness and craft. "Nothing comes cheap nowadays. Why don't you advance her the money? Sheriff makes a pretty good salary."

"Not that good," said Joe, "I guess we'll have to drop the whole idea… Something else I want to ask you about Ken: do you know what girls he'd been going around with?"

"No. That's something he was close as a clam on."

"What about male friends, aside from Bill Whipple?"

"Well, let's see. There'd be Wilson Henderson, Gary Snook, Pete Ravazza, probably a few others. You talk to those boys, they'll steer you to all the others."

Joe copied names, addresses and took his leave.

4

Back at his office Joe made a series of notes.

> Golf course.
> Relations with fellow employees.
> Friends: male, female.
> Bank account.

Rex Kelly appeared and made a report on the day's activities. "First of all, the hammers. I picked up all I could find, and some hatchets as well. None of them test for blood."

Joe gave a gloomy grunt. "It was a long chance to begin with. Take them all back."

"Right. I also worked up a list of all the *Life* subscribers on Ken's route, or, I should say, the addresses of all this week's magazines. I'll compare this with next week's list and maybe we'll learn something."

Joe grunted. "Maybe, maybe not. I've checked along Madrone Way, and everybody seems to be pretty well equipped." He frowned. There was a tickling in his mind. Somewhere along the line he had half-noticed something. What the devil had it been? So much had happened during the day it was hard to keep everything clear.

He frowned down at his list. "Here's what I want you to do tomorrow. Check the golf course, find out who was playing Tuesday morning. Get their names, question them. Item two: visit the post office, talk to the fellows Ken worked with. Item three: go to the bank, check on Ken's account and his monthly statements. That ought to hold you awhile."

"Most of the morning, I'd say."

Joe leaned back in his chair. "I guess you haven't heard the latest: Mrs. Bazzarini says it wasn't Ken who delivered the Mortimer house. She could be wrong, but she thinks it was somebody else."

Rex Kelly's jaw fell slack. "How the hell can that be? A substitute carrier maybe?"

"No. According to the Taylor kids, Ken drove into Madrone Way and never came out. Marsh Shortridge spoke to Ken. After that no one admits talking to Ken. Everybody says their mail was shoved into the box. Mrs. Benjamin did not get her registered letter, Mrs. Bazzarini had no mail at all. What does that mean?"

"It means," said Rex Kelly, "that somebody bashed Ken, then delivered the rest of the mail."

"That's just how I figure."

"It seems a risk. A big risk."

"Not if the murderer got into Ken's uniform," said Joe.

The two men sat silent a moment.

Joe went on. "The killer would have to go on delivering the mail: otherwise the house where the mail stopped would indicate where Ken got killed."

"Assuming that this is the case," said Rex Kelly, "the uniform would have to fit the murderer — at least approximately. Ken was about average height. He had good shoulders, but he was pretty slim otherwise. That lets Caspar Hubman out right there. He could never get his belly into Ken's pants. Mrs. Benjamin, who is remarkably pregnant, also eases out of contention."

Joe scribbled a list of names:

    Sam Shortridge
    Miriam Shortridge
    Marsh Shortridge
    Starr Shortridge
    Tom Taylor
    Sheila Taylor
    Grace Benjamin
    Sally Wagner
    Fred Whipple
    Sheila Whipple
    Bill Whipple
    Caspar Hubman
    Laura Hubman
    Mrs. Cream
    Mrs. Bazzarini
    Barbara Locke

"These are the adult residents of Madrone Way. The two older Shortridges have alibis, as does Tom Taylor and Fred Whipple. Mrs. Taylor could not hide a mail van from her kids; Caspar Hubman is too fat, Mrs. Benjamin is too pregnant. Mrs. Cream is fairly stocky and something other than snow white, which lets her out. Mrs. Bazzarini and Miss Locke vouch for each other. I can't imagine either one chasing after Ken to bang him on the head." Joe crossed out names, prepared a new list:

> Marsh Shortridge
> Starr Shortridge
> Sally Wagner
> Bill Whipple
> Laura Hubman

For a long minute he scrutinized the five names. "All these people could do the job. They could also get into Ken's uniform without looking grotesque. Sally Wagner just barely. Laura Hubman's bottom is also deluxe."

"It seems so reckless!" Rex Kelly exclaimed. "Everybody knows everyone else; just one look and then 'Why hello, Mrs. Wagner, what in the world are you doing in that uniform?'"

"Whoever killed the mailman has to deliver the mail," said Joe. "Otherwise the jig is up. And who looks at the mailman? He's just a piece of the street, like a fire hydrant. The biggest risk was at Mrs. Bazzarini's house — and she didn't get her mail. Mrs. Benjamin likewise did not get her registered letter either."

Rex Kelly nodded dubiously. "In that case the scene of the crime would seem to be located somewhere before the Benjamin house — at the Shortridges' or at the Taylors'."

"True. But my candidate is Bill Whipple." He rose to his feet. "Before you go home I want you to run over to the morgue, give Ken's uniform a close look for hairs or odd-colored lipstick or something of the sort."

"Right, Sheriff."

5

Joe drove out to Madrone Way, parked in front of the Whipple house. He walked up to the door, rang the bell. There was no response.

Joe went back to stand by his car. He looked right and left along Madrone Way, up Spanish Hill. He watched the progress of a late afternoon foursome on the golf course, wondering how long it would be before his mother and Miranda insisted that they all join the country club...If his mother guaranteed to take up golf, it would almost be worth the price.

Sally Wagner, wearing red slacks and a black sweater, came from her house, ostensibly to turn on the lawn sprinklers. She noticed Joe with a little jerk of surprise. "Sheriff Joe Bain! Why are you standing so quietly, with such a sinister expression?"

"You caught me in the act of thinking, Mrs. Wagner."

Mrs. Wagner bent over to adjust the faucet, and Joe mentally held up Ken's trousers against the red-clad expanse. He made a tuneless hissing sound between his teeth, gave his head a skeptical shake. Sally Wagner came down to the sidewalk. "Are there any new developments to the murder case?"

"We're still in the process of getting facts. I've been trying to catch up with Bill Whipple, who seems to have been one of Ken's friends."

Sally Wagner pursed her lips. "I believe they had a falling out of some kind — probably because of their educational differences and so forth. In my opinion Bill is a very arrogant young man. Incidentally, I don't think you'll catch him tonight. Sheila Whipple told me that they were all going into San Jose this evening."

"The morning will do just as well," said Joe. "But back to Ken. You didn't see him at all the other day? Not even a glimpse?"

"No, not a glimpse. Usually he came tramping up the stairs, whistling or singing; he was such a cheerful lad. But Tuesday — not a sound. Perhaps he had something on his mind. Premonition?"

"He was in good humor when the Taylor boys saw him. That was before he went to the Shortridges'."

Sally Wagner rose to the bait. "Perhaps he heard something disturbing at the Shortridges'. They're a strange lot, those young ones. Sam and Miriam are small-town aristocrats, no question there, but their children are absolutely feudal. Marsh looks down his nose at everybody. I'm sure he's unhealthy mentally. He reminds me of the young German army officers in the World War movies — cold-blooded and formal. You know the type. Starr is very different, but she's as proud as they come. They're both utter snobs. I've had only the barest civility from either of the two… Poor little Alice Benjamin, marrying into such a family! It's a shame!"

"How so?"

"I shouldn't say this, because it's sheer conjecture, but if you ask me, Grace Benjamin pushed Alice into it. Grace is an ambitious woman, for all her religion. You know she's a fervent Irish Catholic, which means no birth control. I suppose she feels self-conscious, which is all very well, but —" In vivid detail Sally Wagner described her quarrel with Grace Benjamin. "We've never really been cordial since."

"Sometimes that's the way things work out," said Joe. "What kind of a man is Mr. Benjamin?"

"He's a dear!" declared Sally Wagner. "Perhaps a little too easy-going. Alice has her father's disposition, and I'm afraid Grace has ruled them both with an iron hand." She turned to look after a passing car. "Somebody for the Hubmans. I'm a dreadful scandal-monger, I know, but I find people so interesting and I can't resist talking about them. But won't you come in for a glass of sherry? It's just about that time."

Joe glanced at the sun, which was touching the trees, checked it against his watch. "No, thanks, I'd better be starting home."

"Some other time then."

6

During dinner Miranda proposed a system for decorating the bedrooms at Halfway House: "They could all be different colors! There'd be a Red Room and a Green Room and a Blue Room — and everything in the rooms would be red and green and blue."

Marian Bain frowned. "Who would want to sleep in a Purple Room? Or a Black Room? Don't forget, there are ten rooms."

Joe said dourly, "Forget it, girls. Maybe Halfway House isn't such a good idea after all."

Miranda looked at him with a stricken face. "Oh Daddy!"

Joe's mother exclaimed: "What? You traipse us out there, you get us all excited, and now, cool as you please, you decide it's not a good idea?"

Joe looked from daughter to mother with a slack jaw. "Well — in the first place, Clarence Mooney wants an impossible price."

"Just what is 'impossible'?"

"His first figure — forty grand."

"That certainly seems out of reach," Marian Bain conceded reluctantly. "Do you think the place is worth it?"

"Maybe, maybe not. I haven't given up. But right now this killing is on my mind and it's all I can think of."

"Do you know who did it, Daddy?"

"Yeah. Somebody along Madrone Way. That's as close as I can come. I've asked every question I can think of, but naturally the guilty party is giving me careful answers...Well, something will turn up."

Chapter VIII

Friday morning began poorly. There was a particularly heavy load of routine work and Miss Curdy seemed more obtuse than ever.

At ten o'clock Constable William White called in from Vogelburg to request assistance. Two miles south of Vogelburg was the Dedrick dairy farm, where, during the morning milking, a Swiss farm-hand had run amok. Seizing an axe, he had split the skulls of nine Jerseys and two Holsteins, then had chased Mrs. Dedrick down the road. Returning to the bunkhouse and arming himself with a .22 rifle, he had climbed to the top of a silo where he now stood at bay, shooting at everything in sight.

Summoning Deputies Ben Boso and Fay Insley, Joe drove to the Dedrick farm. The road was lined with parked cars, and a hundred persons of all ages and sexes stood watching.

Joe instructed Constable White to establish road-blocks and divert traffic, then set himself to a consideration of the problem. How to bring the maniac down from the silo without bloodshed?

Joe brought forth a bullhorn and called up to the unseen man, urging him to throw down his rifle and descend. In response came a *spanggg-thwack*! as the maniac attempted to expunge the source of the noise.

Joe drew back, and stood scowling at the silo. The covert grins of the onlookers began to make Joe fretful, as did the suggestions which were put forward: "Call for a helicopter, blow the guy off with a gust!" "Use tear gas!" "Wash him down with a fire hose!"

Joe controlled his temper. If he bawled orders and reprimands, he'd lose votes. If he failed to produce, he'd also lose votes. What would old Cooch have done in a case like this? Old Cooch would never have come out here in the first place, Joe thought glumly. He'd have sent Deputy Joe Bain.

A man in a brown suit and a wide-brimmed straw hat came forward. "I'm Les Druper, Vogelburg correspondent for the *Messenger*. What do you think about all this, Sheriff?"

"I think it's a ticklish situation, especially for the guy on the silo."

"What do you propose to do?"

Joe considered a moment. "Well, I could go up there after him. He'd shoot me, then jump to the ground and two maniacs would be dead. I'm going to try to psyche him down."

"How's that?"

"Just watch." Joe signaled Deputies Boso and Insley. "I want everybody to clear out. Get all these people back into their cars and send them home. I want the road absolutely clear."

The order was easier to issue than to execute, but half an hour later the road was clear. The spectators had departed, along with William Dedrick, his wife, Les Druper, Constable William White, Deputies Boso and Insley and Joe himself.

The farm and the surrounding countryside were deserted. The sun beat down on the silo. The maniac was puzzled. He looked this way and that. No one in sight. He raised his head and listened. No sound except the rustle of the breeze in the eucalyptus trees. He shot two chickens. No one seemed to care.

The top of the silo was hot. After half an hour, he became disgusted and descended the ladder. He looked uncertainly this way and that. Never had the farm seemed so silent — except on Sunday mornings, when Mr. and Mrs. Dedrick went to church in Vogelburg. Sunday morning? Could it possibly be Sunday morning? What was he doing out here in the hot sun? The maniac went into the bunkhouse.

From a nearby barn Joe had been watching through binoculars. Boso and Insley had made a wide circuit and were now at the back of an alfalfa field, lying in an irrigation ditch. Joe called them on his transceiver. Sheltered from view by the Dedrick farmhouse, they ran forward and took up stations at opposite corners of the house.

Joe now left the barn. Sidling along the road, he approached the bunkhouse, tossed a tear-gas grenade through the window. The maniac rushed out and was immediately captured by Boso and Insley.

Constable White removed the road-blocks; the folk of the neighborhood returned to marvel at the silo and commiserate with the Dedricks over the dead cows.

Boso and Insley took the captive off to Pleasant Grove. Joe went to his car and radioed headquarters. Ace Wardell had nothing urgent to communicate. There had been no breaks in the Mooney case. Rex Kelly had left a memorandum to the effect that, first, he had interrogated Bill Whipple, learning nothing of significance; and second, he had gleaned no clues from an inspection of Ken Mooney's uniform.

Joe started back toward Pleasant Grove, and decided that while he was in the neighborhood he might as well drop by the Mooney ranch. In the course of talking among themselves, the Mooneys might have recalled a significant fact. Conceivably Clarence Mooney had recalculated the price of Halfway House.

Joe drove southwest to Coyote, then cut off through the hills down to Oatfarm Road and presently turned into the Mooney driveway.

No one was home. The afternoon sun baked the house. In the front yard a few stunted hollyhocks were wilting. The windmill creaked and groaned like a lost soul.

Joe stood a moment looking at the house, wondering how people could live in a situation so barren and bleak when there wasn't any real need for it... Somber and depressed, he continued south to Hankinson Road. He paused at the sign PANDORA REALTY, looked in toward the house, but saw only the shimmer of thought-focusing tanks. The car was gone; no one seemed to be home. Joe felt more cheerless than ever. "I could even use some of that tea."

Two miles down the road he came upon a stalled car, with a woman struggling to change a flat tire. Joe pulled over to the side; here was a vote for sure, and maybe that of her husband as well. It never hurt to act like a gentleman.

The woman stood up; Joe saw her to be Luna, from the planet Arthemisia. Today she wore the garments of Earth: a simple brown and white cotton frock, and once again Joe could not help but notice how closely her attributes matched Earthly standards of beauty. Joe's spirits rose. He jumped from the car; Luna wiped her forehead gratefully, leaving a rather appealing smear of dirt. "I'm so glad to see you, Sheriff! I detest these flat things."

"I'm glad I wandered by," said Joe. "Now if you'll just stand to the side and admire my skill…"

Joe jacked up the car, removed the tire, only to discover that the spare was also flat.

Luna was perplexed. "I can't imagine where all the air went. It was full when I bought the car."

"There's only one thing to do," said Joe. "We'll take the tires into town and have them refilled. It might take some little time. Were you going any place in a big hurry?"

"Well, no. Just some shopping."

Joe loaded the tires into the back of his car, helped Luna into the front seat, and continued along Hankinson Road.

At the highway intersection Joe turned north toward Aurora, where he had few acquaintances. At the outskirts of town he stopped at a service station, dropped off the tires for repair.

"Things get pretty busy this time of day," Joe told Luna. "There'll be a wait… It's still a bit early for dinner; let's have a drink or two."

Luna made no protest and Joe drove to the Black Bull, Aurora's most distinguished restaurant. Before alighting he checked into headquarters. "Sheriff Bain here. Anything going on?"

"Pretty quiet," said Ace Wardell.

"Good. I'd like you to call home for me, say I've been unavoidably detained and not to wait dinner."

"Right, Sheriff, will do."

"If anything comes up, I'm at the Black Bull in Aurora."

Joe escorted Luna to a booth in the bar section, ordered her a frozen daiquiri and himself a highball. "Here we are," said Joe. "I can think of worse things to be doing."

"Yes," said Luna, in a voice which for some reason had become prim. "It's very nice in here. How long will it be before the tires are fixed?"

Joe raised his eyebrows, wondering what he had done to exasperate her. "Heavens, I don't know. A couple hours, I suppose. But drink up. How are the thought-control pans working out?"

"Not too well. Something is causing a false vibration. I'm afraid the system isn't practical."

"You never know till you try," said Joe. "I could use some thought-wave equipment…Maybe it's just as well I don't. The jail is crowded now."

"Earth is a chaotic world," said Luna.

"It's got its good points," said Joe, "but you have to have a swift personality to take advantage of them. If I ever get rich it'll be by accident. I don't suppose the real estate business is all that good either."

Luna shook her head, smiling at Joe's naïveté. "I have never needed to concern myself. In Texas I was given wealth by someone I helped."

The conversation proceeded. Luna's coolness gradually disappeared and after her second daiquiri she was leaning forward, her great dark eyes eager and attentive. Joe was discussing the Mooney case: "I don't mind being baffled if there's a fighting chance of enlightenment. Here in this miserable case there's no way to turn. Nobody knows anything; everybody insinuates that his neighbour is a boor, but that's as far as they're willing to go."

Luna thoughtfully inspected the bottom of her glass and Joe signaled the waitress for a third round. "The use of a hammer implies a crime of sudden fury," said Luna. "Fury or panic. A crime without premeditation. The hammer must have been close at hand. Were any of your suspects building anything?"

Joe scratched his nose. "I didn't think to ask…It's a good point. I ought to sign you up as a special detective."

Luna shook her head. "I would never know how to deal with hate or avarice."

"It's hard to avoid," said Joe. "How did you ever manage to buy a car?"

Luna shrugged. "There are many systems. I use a small crystal orb on a silver chain, and swing it back and forth."

"Oh? Does it help?"

"If it doesn't, I go to another agency."

Joe sipped his highball. "Back to Ken Mooney, something else looms up through the fog. I've been asking myself: was Ken demolished because he was the mailman or because he was Ken? In other words, was the motive associated with his work or his private life? The hammer, as you point out, shows lack of premeditation, and this would indicate murder of the mailman. If Ken was murdered in his own identity, the killer would probably have planned something more elegant."

"There might have been a sudden argument," Luna pointed out. "Or perhaps each day Ken Mooney compounded a small offense, and suddenly drove someone past the edge of restraint."

Joe threw up his hands in defeat. "Every time I think I'm deriving order from the confusion, somebody pulls the string. Incidentally, let me wipe that smear of grease off your face. People have been looking at you rather funny."

Luna jumped to her feet. "Why didn't you tell me?"

"I didn't think about it," said Joe.

Luna marched to the ladies' room. When she returned Joe escorted her into the restaurant. "The steaks here are usually pretty good. I suddenly remember I didn't have any lunch, what with William Dedrick and his mad help. I plan to dine."

Luna for a moment or two returned to her mysterious mood of cool withdrawal; nevertheless she did not reject the menu which Joe put into her hands. Over steak, onion rings and Monteverde Pinot Noir, Luna once again became cordial.

Joe indicated the wine. "Every time we tilt that bottle we enrich Mrs. Bazzarini, who would be one of my prime suspects except that she's a helpless invalid and she loved Ken like a son. Also, a nurse watches her every move. I tend to eliminate Mrs. Bazzarini. Some of the others have alibis; some are too pregnant; some are too fat. There aren't many suspects left."

"One might consider the crime an illusion."

"Unfortunately not. Coffee?"

"No, thank you."

"The evening is young," said Joe. "I don't know what your social habits are, but what do you say to taking your car home and then checking out a bottle of Scotch?"

Luna raised her expressive eyebrows. Her voice again was cool. "Hadn't you better call your wife first?"

All was now clear. Joe chuckled. "That would be a thankless task. Sixteen years ago she ran off with a guitar player. Presumably the relationship no longer applies. What about you?"

"Arthemisians have customs different from those of Earth."

"I'd like to hear about them," said Joe. He paid the check, bought a bottle of Scotch at the bar. At the service station he picked up the tires; returning along Hankinson Road to Luna's car, he mounted the repaired tire, replaced the spare in its well.

The summer days were long; when they arrived at Luna's cottage afterglow still colored the west.

Luna brought a table up to the lawn swing, fetched ice, water, glasses. Then she went inside again and returned in a loose sheer frock. Joe thought she looked wonderfully cool and fresh.

Joe opened the bottle, poured. "I'm certainly glad Mr. Rank asked me to drop by here. Do you know why?"

"No," said Luna archly. "Why?"

"Well, if he hadn't, and if we were sitting here like this, the night would have been thick with mosquitos."

"Well yes. I suppose that's true."

"Also, I might not have been here at all."

"Many things are beyond comprehension."

"I could name a dozen," said Joe. "Two dozen. At the moment I refuse to even think about Ken Mooney."

"It's much too nice an evening."

The level in the bottle sagged; the afterglow waned, the stars came forth. Luna pointed. "See up there…No, there…That's the direction of Arthemisia, in the constellation Virgo."

"I won't ask how you arrived," said Joe. "In the first place, without a passport, it's illegal."

Luna smiled thoughtfully up toward the stars. Joe trickled whiskey over ice, added water, rattled the glass to make a pleasant tinkling. "Do they do much drinking up there?"

Luna nodded. "Elixirs, essences derived from fruit blossoms."

"It sounds nice. What do they do for entertainment?"

"Oh — sing, recite sagas, walk along the beaches."

"What about their love-life?"

Luna reflected a moment. "I guess it's about like here."

"For instance, they hold hands about like this?"

"Oh, yes."

"And maybe take hold of each other about like this?"

"Well, yes. About like that."

"And then they…"

"…Well…"

"And then…"

"Joe, be careful. This is only gauze…"

"…good heavens, what on earth is that?"

"Just something all the girls on Arthemisia wear."

"…yeah. Now I get the hang of it…"

"…"

"…Luna."

"Yes, Joe?"

"Nothing, really." Joe swirled ice around in his glass. "It's so nice out here…I hate to think about going back to the world of the real."

Luna looked up toward Virgo and Spica and the star Vindemiatrix by the Lair of the Howling Dog. "You're much too conscientious."

"I've got to be something. It appears that I'm not smart. Right now there's a killer laughing up his sleeve. I have the terrible suspicion he's laughing at me…Can I pour for you?"

"No, thanks."

"I guess you never knew Ken? He lived only a mile or two up the road."

"I know his father. He has a property listed with me."

"Oh? Which property is this?"

"An old hotel over toward Jordan. He's a very peculiar man to deal with."

"I agree as to that," said Joe. "What's his price?"

"That's what's so peculiar. It was twenty-eight thousand, then he came down to twenty-six five, then yesterday he told me to hold off for a few days because he had a hot prospect on the hook."

"Hmmf." Joe sat up in the lawn swing, put his glass down on the table. "While I'm in the vicinity I better go up and talk to Mooney."

Luna sighed. "It's such a beautiful evening."

"It certainly is," said Joe. "But that's the way it goes."

Joe drove up Oatfarm Road, turned into the Mooney driveway. There were lights in the tall box of a house, and Clarence Mooney's spare shape was silhouetted as he came to peer out the screen door.

Joe stepped out of the car. "Hi there, Mr. Mooney."

"Oh. It's you, Sheriff."

"I happened to be driving past and I thought I'd talk to you for a bit."

"Sure thing. I won't ask you in; the wife and girls are watching TV."

"You haven't thought of anything more in connection with Ken?"

"Not a thing, Sheriff. Except that I feel sure it was a ghastly mistake."

"There's always that chance. Have you had a chance to go into Ken's finances?"

Mooney nodded. "He didn't have any to speak of. There was government insurance, which he'd made out to his mother."

"Have you come across any letters or diaries, or memorandum books — anything which might give us a hint?"

"Not a single thing."

"Hmmf...Well, I'll be driving on. Incidentally, about Halfway House, my mother changed her mind. She thinks the place is too far gone. She doesn't want to go much more than fifteen thousand. I said I'd throw in another thousand, so your feelings wouldn't be hurt too bad, but that's her final stone-wall non-elastic offer."

Clarence Mooney started to speak, but the words caught in his throat. Finally he said, "I don't think we can do much business."

"Probably just as well for all concerned," said Joe. "Well, goodnight."

Mooney turned on his heel and strode into the house.

Joe drove back to the Pandora Realty. Luna came to the door.

"It's me again," called Joe. "I've got some business for you." He wrote a check for a thousand dollars. "Wait a day or so, then call Mr. Mooney and tell him you think you can unload Halfway House for twenty-six five. If he says yes, write him your own check for a thousand as a deposit. Specify that the selling price must include the property, appurtenances and contents, all the old knickknacks. Under no circumstances mention my name. Out of sheer excitement he might not want to sell."

CHAPTER IX

1

JOE READ THE FRIDAY EDITION of the *Messenger* over his bacon and
eggs. Prominently displayed was an account of the maniac on William
Dedrick's silo. Joe read the story with disbelief. Nowhere were the craft
and finesse of Sheriff Joe Bain celebrated. Instead:

> Sheriff Joe Bain hid in a barn until the maniac descended from
> the silo. Sheriff's Deputies Ben Boso and Fay Insley finally made
> the arrest.

Joe flung the paper to the floor and was reprimanded by his mother,
who did not approve of emotional excess.

Joe retrieved the paper, and read further. There was an article in
connection with the Mooney murder, offensive only because of its
accuracy:

> Sheriff Joe Bain announces that the investigation is proceed-
> ing, but that so far no definite leads exist.

The telephone rang; Joe answered. "Joe Bain speaking."

"Rex Kelly here. Nothing doing at the golf course: nobody in the
foursome that was playing Tuesday morning noticed a thing out of the
way. I also talked to Bill Whipple; he says he's just as puzzled about
Ken's death as everybody else. He says Ken had no enemies, no debts,
and as far as he knew was in good spirits. He claims he hadn't seen
much of Ken recently. He can offer no alibi and doesn't take seriously

the idea that he might be a suspect. He certainly doesn't act like one. In fact he's the most cocksure guy I've run into for a long time."

2

Bill Whipple jumped down the front steps and out into Madrone Way where his Corvette was parked. Bill was tall, broad-shouldered, nervously muscular, thin in the flanks, long of leg. He carried his head high, somewhat flung back; his eyes darted restlessly, this way and that, with the alert vigilance of a hawk: a resemblance heightened by the bony structure of his face, the harsh narrow nose, the thin crooked mouth. Bill Whipple was far from handsome, but he attracted and fascinated the eye. Bill Whipple was born out of his time. Three thousand years ago he might have been a barbarian hero; five hundred years ago, a Renaissance prince. Today Bill Whipple sold used cars on his father's lot.

Climbing into his car he noticed Starr Shortridge leaving her driveway with a tennis racket, evidently bound for the country club.

Bill gunned the Corvette into life and was almost instantly alongside her. "Hey Starr!"

Starr turned Bill a glance of puzzled inquiry, as if she were not sure whether or not she knew him.

Bill vaulted from the car, stood facing her. "Where are you going?"

"To play tennis."

"I've got a better idea. I'll take you uptown and buy you a big double chocolate ice cream soda." He stood back, looked Starr up and down. Starr was wearing dark brown shorts, a blue and white striped polo shirt. "Come to think of it," said Bill, "you even look like a double chocolate ice cream soda, with whipped cream."

For a fact, Starr looked her best. Her hair was loose and glossy, her skin was tan and glistened with a healthy sheen.

"What about it?" asked Bill. Already his voice was a trifle unsure, a tone or two high in pitch: an effect no other girl had ever been able to achieve. Starr was an abstraction as well as a girl: a goal, a destiny, and he hated her as much as he yearned for her. "Jump in. This thing flies. It'll be chocolate ice cream sodas while we're hardly thinking about them. I've got a lot to talk to you about. Two hundred items of great interest."

Starr took a slow step away, watching Bill sidewise. He has a reptile's eye, she thought: bold, unafraid, the gaze all external. Her skin tingled. The atavistic response was still in operation; her nerves sent unintelligible messages to her brain. Starr took another step along the street. "No thanks. I really don't care for an ice cream soda." With a vague half-smile she turned away.

A sudden passion came over Bill; he took a lunging step forward, seized her elbow, swung her around so that once again she faced him.

Starr's face conveyed only mild surprise, hardly even annoyance: as if a dog had barked at her from behind a fence. Bill felt the import of the blank expression and became more irritated than ever. He wanted to provoke her to emotion — some emotion, any emotion. "I'll tell you something. From the first time I saw you, when you were tearing down my tree-house —" He stopped short, disconcerted by Starr's unresponsiveness.

Starr, for her part, was conscious only of her archaic female instincts: a situation which repelled and disgusted her. She detached herself from Bill's grasp. "If you don't mind —"

"Just a minute!" cried Bill. "I want to know something. Do you really dislike me, or is this just an act, a put-on?"

Starr found the remark mirth-provoking. "I'm not conscious of any act, or 'put-on'. Now, if you'll please excuse me."

Bill stood with shoulders drooping, arms dangling by his sides — defeated, reduced to querulousness. "What is it about me you dislike?"

"I've never given the matter any thought," said Starr, with a cool candor that was totally convincing. She walked away, twitching her tennis racket.

Bill stood stiff as a post, staring after the slender, somewhat boyish figure in brown shorts. "Teaser!" he whispered huskily. "Oh what a teaser!" He took two quick steps after her, then checked himself, jumped into his Corvette and raced off down Madrone Way at breakneck speed. Starr hardly bothered to glance after him, so Bill, craning his neck as he swung around the turn into McClellan Avenue, noticed. If Starr had wished to focus Bill's attention on herself, she could not have succeeded more completely. Whispering fervent curses, Bill considered schemes to get his own back. There must be some way to make her aware of him! He had tried something of the sort before, but it had failed to work. Of course he had not used the whole of his power. Power! If not to construct, then to destroy! Why not? Why not, indeed?

3

Joe, restless and nervous as a shoplifter, drove to headquarters. There were no female prisoners, Miss Curdy was not in the office; the atmosphere on this account seemed unusually tranquil and suave.

Joe went to his office, leaned back in his chair, put his feet on the desk. So far as he could see, the Mooney case had reached a dead-end. The murder, on the face of it, seemed irrational. Perhaps something to do with Halfway House? Even as Joe considered the matter, the telephone rang. Luna's clear voice emerged from the speaker. "Joe? If you remember, we discussed a certain property near Jordan?"

"I remember distinctly."

"Well, half an hour ago the owner dropped by and put the listing back on active! I told him that I might be able to sell for twenty-six five, and he agreed to accept the offer. I gave him a thousand dollars deposit, my check; and the deal is closed."

"You mean it's definite? I'm the owner?"

"Subject to paying the balance within forty-five days."

"That's feasible, provided everything goes well at the bank. I'll make arrangements first thing Monday morning. You didn't mention my name to Mooney?"

"No."

"Wise girl … I'll give you a call tomorrow. Maybe even tonight."

"Not tonight, Joe. I'm going to San Jose for a meeting of the Pansophist Society."

The conversation at an end, Joe sat back in his chair. So now: Halfway House. As if there were not enough on his mind already.

He telephoned the news to his mother. "As of now we own twenty acres of land, together with a beat-up old tavern. The liquor license will be registered to you." Joe grinned at the squawk of protest. "That's the way it has to be. It wouldn't look good for the sheriff to be a bartender on the side. Miranda is far too young. That leaves you."

"I never, never thought I'd see the day when I was owner of a bar," declared Marian Bain feelingly. "I certainly don't know what I'll tell my friends!"

"Invite them all out for the grand opening. Where's Miranda?"

"Where do you expect? Primping in the bathroom."

"Let's go inspect our new property. The price is so low I figure I must have made a terrible mistake."

"I can't go, not today. Dora Larkin is taking me to San Rodrigo to see Aunt Ellen."

"Ask Miranda if she wants to go."

Marian Bain called to Miranda, received a reply. "She says yes."

"Tell her to be ready." Joe hung up the telephone, jumped to his feet. "I might as well be roving the countryside; I'm doing no good around here."

4

Halfway House looked much as it had before, with an important distinction. Where previously the air of quiet decrepitude had seemed quaint and nostalgic, now it represented expense. "Good Lord!" said Joe. "I didn't realize the place was so far gone! I fear that Clarence Mooney stuck me badly."

"Oh come now, Daddy," said Miranda. "It's nothing near that bad. In fact it's the most picturesque old place I've ever seen!"

"You're not noticing the toil. Look at those shingles! I'll have to get a new roof on first thing. Look at that blistered paint up there on the balcony!"

"Heavens, Daddy, you mustn't be afraid of a little work! I'll paint the balcony. I'll get Fred and Emmett and Ronald to help. They'll work like crazy — at least Fred and Ronald will. Emmett's pretty lazy."

"Look at the porch," said Joe. "I think it's sagging."

"That's easy to fix. Just jack it up and put a rock under those wooden post-things."

"You make it sound so simple."

Wilbur Baker appeared. "Hey there, Sheriff."

"Hello Wilbur. Open this place up, will you? You're looking at the new owner."

"Well, well. How in the world did you ever deal with Clarence?"

"He gave me a tussle. He still doesn't know who he sold to."

Wilbur Baker nodded glumly. "I guess you don't need me around here any more. I want to go back to Missouri and live with my son. Ken needed someone to help him out; he had no sense. He got in with a no-good crowd. All they cared about was hell-raising and sleeping together. Fair made me sick. Some of them girls, I swear, was not even out of school."

As before, Joe attempted to elicit details, but Wilbur Baker could or would give none. "It was his place; he could do as he liked. I kept away when he was having a party."

"How many parties did he have?"

Wilbur Baker was becoming confused and disturbed. "I couldn't tell you. Maybe half a dozen. I can't see why you're so interested. He ain't had a party since last winter."

"It probably doesn't make any difference," said Joe. "Well, if you want to open up, I think I'll take a look around."

"Here," growled Wilbur Baker. "You're the owner, take the keys. I'll probably be gone next time you show up."

"Stay on as long as you like," said Joe. "Don't hurry off on my account."

With a grudging nod Wilbur Baker stumped off to his quarters. Joe and Miranda opened the doors wide, roamed the old inn from attic to kitchen closets. The previous owners had thrown nothing away; everywhere were relics of the past: mementoes, trophies, curios. Old photographs bedecked the mirror of the bar; on the walls hung antlers, walrus tusks, a bear's head, Indian baskets. In the attic were a dozen ancient suitcases, packed for journeys long forgotten. "This is spooky up here," said Miranda. "Let's go back downstairs."

"We'll want to check these suitcases pretty carefully," said Joe. "We might find a hoard of Indian-head pennies, or even some Kennedy half-dollars."

"Or a Gutenberg Bible."

"More likely just a lot of dirty old corsets," said Joe. "That's about all Clarence Mooney would have allowed to remain."

They looked through the old bedrooms, which were floored with biscuit-colored linoleum and empty except for dead flies and a random scatter of newspapers.

"Ten new beds, ten new mattresses," said Joe. "Ten rugs, ten chairs, ten chamberpots, twenty gallons of paint. I guess I'll put you and your grandmother in charge of everything around here. I'm too frail."

"Oh Daddy! You're being silly. Things aren't all that bad! We'll do one room at a time. It'll be fun!"

"I hope so," said Joe. "I can just hear your grandmother when some-body criticizes her cooking."

"I think we should just serve pizza."

"For breakfast, lunch and dinner? I'd better send you on a tour of the world's great restaurants to check on what's done. In fact, we'll all go... I better go console Wilbur Baker so that he doesn't set fire to the place as a parting gesture."

"I'm going to work, right now," said Miranda. "To start with I'll sweep the lobby."

"Don't burn yourself out."

Joe went off to the combination garage and stable, fifty yards to the rear, where he found a decaying buggy, an old Marmon roadster sup-ported on blocks, several desiccated saddles, crates of bottles, boxes of assorted junk. In the old hostler's quarters Wilbur Baker made his residence.

"Hey, Mr. Baker!" called Joe. "Can I talk to you a minute?"

Wilbur Baker appeared. "What can I do for you?"

"I don't know where the corners to the property are. I wonder if you could point them out to me. Also I'd like to look over the water supply."

"There's a road up to the water tank. We might as well drive your automobile. It's a good walk for an old man."

Joe and Wilbur Baker drove off to inspect the water tank and the corner markers. Hardly had they left when into the driveway skidded a white Corvette driven by a hawk-faced young man with a pinched pale mouth and a shock of short sandy hair. He swung the Corvette to a quivering halt, jumped out all in a single motion. For a moment he stood swaying as if intoxicated by the rhythm of the vehicle. He looked along the façade of Halfway House. Noting the open door, he ran up the steps, entered the lobby.

Miranda, cleaning fly-specks from the mirror behind the desk, turned in surprise. She wondered at the intensity of his expression. He looked like someone keyed up for a desperate venture.

Bill Whipple stood stock-still in the doorway. "Who are you?"

"The new owner," said Miranda saucily. "Who are you?"

Bill did not reply directly. "So Mooney let the place go. Wicked old son of a bitch." He stepped forward. "I'm a friend of Ken's. I came for one or two things that he gave to me."

"Oh?" Secure in the knowledge that her father, the important Sheriff Joe Bain, was close at hand, Miranda decided to tease this dangerous-looking young man. "Just what 'things' are these?"

"Just a few odds and ends." He looked past her. "Are you alone here?"

Miranda wondered what might have happened if, in fact, she had been alone. "My father's around somewhere."

"Where?"

"I don't know." Miranda turned to look out the door past Bill's shoulder. "If his car's not there, he must have driven off for a few minutes."

"I see. Is the bar open?"

"Not for business. You'd better wait for my father."

"I can't wait. I'm in a rush." Bill went to the handsome mahogany and glass doors between lobby and dining room, pushed them ajar, stepped through. Miranda gave a yelp of protest and went after him, across the dining room, into the bar.

Bill stood in the center of the room, looking around with an expression of sardonic self-pity. "Since I have the reputation," Bill told himself, "I might as well be one."

"Please get out of here!" said Miranda firmly.

Bill went behind the bar, picked up a whisky bottle with two inches remaining. "See this bottle?" He held it up. "Mine. I brought it out here."

"You leave things alone!" declared Miranda in outrage.

"How about a drink, kid? What's your name?"

"Miranda Bain. And I don't want a drink. I want you to get out of here."

Bill took a leisurely taste of his own whisky, looked around the walls. His eyes focused on a photograph; he crossed the room, began to disengage the photograph.

"Don't you dare do that!" cried Miranda. "Those are part of the decorations!"

"Not all of them. Some are mine."

"You'll have to talk to my father about things like that."

"I thought you were the owner," said Bill, tucking the picture into his pocket.

"Never mind what I am. Give me that picture."

Bill looked Miranda up and down: slender legs, hips, elastic torso, thin vivacious face, glossy dark brown hair.

"You know something?" said Bill in wonder. "You're a pretty little dickens. I like you."

"I don't like you."

"That's the story of my life," said Bill. "Almost." To tease Miranda, he turned to take another photograph. She stepped in front of him, a dangerous move, for it brought the two bodies into contact. Bill's hair-trigger disposition needed no further provocation. He put his arms around her, aimed for her mouth, kissed her cheek. Miranda jerked away, seething. Bill came a step forward, grinning. Miranda seized the bottle. "You better stop!" She raised the bottle.

Bill laughed. "You little devil, I believe you mean it."

He stepped forward, evaded the bottle with the ease of long prac-tice, took the bottle away, which meant that he was forced to put his arms around her again. "How about a kiss? Nice, this time."

Miranda fought loose. She had never been so angry in her life. She ran outside, went to the Corvette, snatched out the keys, tossed them under the steps. She marched back to the bar, to find Bill carefully inspecting the photographs.

"You'd better give me that picture," said Miranda, "or you'll be here a long time."

"So? How? Why?"

"I took the keys to your car."

"You did?" Bill stood looking at her. A trifle young, but pretty and passionate. And antagonistic. And female. And pretty. His mouth was a trifle dry. He felt excited. If she took his keys and came back to tell him about it, she could only mean it as a provocation. Well, Bill was game. It seemed like fun. She wouldn't act that way if she expected her father right back. Bill jumped forward, seized her. "Where are the keys?" He searched the pocket in her skirt, reached down inside her blouse. Miranda kicked and tried to bite.

"Give me the keys," said Bill, "or I'll have to search you real careful."

"They're under the porch," gasped Miranda. "You'll be in trouble when my father gets back!"

"'Trouble'?" Bill laughed. "I haven't done a thing. You've made all the trouble. I came to regain some personal property. You tried to brain me with a bottle, then you took my car keys. That's illegal."

"It is not!" Miranda, leaning back against the bar, tried to punch him in the face. Bill, pushing close to her, was impelled past the edge of his precarious restraint.

"What's going on here?" called Joe, who had been attracted by the noise. He jumped forward, grabbed Bill's collar, pulled him back. In one easy motion Bill turned, swung, struck Joe on the jaw, sent him stumbling back.

"You laid hands on me, fella," said Bill. "That's called battery."

"This is called assault," said Joe.

"And this is called a punch in the nose," said Bill.

There was confusion, the thresh of blows, the scuff of feet, the hiss of breath. Joe was cagy and cool, veteran of a hundred brawls with drunks and recalcitrants; Bill was quick and rangy, strong and wild. He hit Joe in the belly; Joe swung sidewise; Bill hit Joe on the cheek, decking him again. Joe caught hold of Bill's leg, heaved, sent him hopping and reeling backwards.

"Hit him again, Daddy!" cried Miranda.

"'Again'?" jeered Bill. "He hasn't come near me."

"Try this one on," said Joe, and he hit Bill a clout on the ear.

Bill in a fury caught hold of Joe's arm, slung him skidding across the dance floor into a corner. Then he turned a table over on Joe, piled on another table, chairs, more tables and chairs, until Joe was trapped in the corner, roaring and cursing, behind a big tangle of furniture.

Bill stood back, pleased with the effect. "If this is the way you treat your customers I won't be back." He patted Miranda on the head. "Goodby cutie. I'll see you again when your old man's not around." He went outside, looked under the steps, found his keys. Now he noticed the black and white official car. He sagged, looked back in astonishment toward the bar. "Miranda *Bain*? Sheriff Joe Bain? Good God! I've cooked my goose for sure!" He jumped into his Corvette and with wheels churning up dirt departed the premises.

Joe crawled out from behind the furniture, ran his hand over his hair, limped out to look after the vanishing car. "Now who in the world was that?"

"He said he was a friend of Ken's," said Miranda, half-sobbing. "He wanted some pictures, and I think he took one — a snapshot, from behind the bar."

"What pictures was he after?"

Miranda pointed to the pictures Bill had started to detach.

"Just those old cars?" asked Joe in bewilderment. "All that trouble for just a few pictures? I can hardly believe it."

"He wasn't serious about those pictures there. He was just trying to tease me, because I told him to leave everything alone." She looked at her reflection in the mirror and shivered. "He's a wild man."

"He didn't tell you his name?"

"No. But when I took the keys from his car I looked at the registration. His name is William Whipple."

"Bill Whipple," cried Joe. "I should have known. I've been trying to get hold of him for days."

"You finally did," said Miranda.

Joe turned her a suspicious side-glance. Miranda's gaze was limpid and clear. "Yes," said Joe, rubbing his face. "We had quite a party."

"Are you going to arrest him?"

Joe sighed. "I'd only make a fool of myself. Under all those chairs yet...Don't worry. I'll have a word or two with him. In fact, right away."

Going out to the car Joe radioed headquarters and instructed Casey Miggs, the deputy on standby duty, to bring Bill Whipple into the office. "He just left Halfway House in a white Corvette, probably coming into Pleasant Grove by Contreras Road and Highway 198."

5

Joe dropped Miranda off at home, went to his office, alternately dictated letters into a recorder and fretted about the Mooney case.

The afternoon passed. Casey Miggs returned without Bill Whipple. "He either drove west on 198 or south on Contreras Road."

Joe telephoned the Whipple residence and Whipple Chevrolet, but received no information as to the whereabouts of Bill Whipple.

At four o'clock, just as Joe was about to close up and go home, he received a visitor: Howard Griselda. Joe affably pushed out a chair, leaned back in his own chair.

Griselda, in no hurry to state the reason for his visit, lit his pipe, looking meanwhile at Joe from under his thick black eyebrows.

Joe became uneasy. "Well, Howard, to what do I owe the honor of this visit?"

"First of all, Sheriff, I'm wondering if you have anything new on the Mooney killing."

"Yes, I think you could say there's been progress."

"You have a suspect?"

Joe frowned. "I wouldn't go so far as to say that. I've eliminated a number of people from consideration. I don't have anything definite pointing to any one person."

Griselda nodded ponderously, blew forth a gust of smoke. Joe continued. "I think it's pretty clear what happened. Whoever killed Ken knew they'd have to deliver the mail all along the street, otherwise where the mail stopped would be a dead giveaway. So the killer changed into Ken's uniform, delivered the mail, at least as far as the Bazzarini house. Then he drove the van into a garage, changed back into normal clothes and waited till dark. That's the way it was done. Pretty clever too."

"Very clever. This morning I received an anonymous phone call. A woman, fairly well educated, or so I'd judge. She suggested that I try to find out where Mrs. Bazzarini was leaving her money."

Joe frowned. "I wonder why she didn't call me... Maybe she was afraid I'd recognize her voice."

"That might be the case."

Joe made a note. "Thanks for the tip. I'll check right away."

Griselda inspected the bowl of his pipe, knocked out the dottle, reloaded it. "I understand that you are planning to buy and operate a roadhouse."

Joe stared at Griselda with raised eyebrows. "How in the world did this news get to you? I've hardly had time to think about it myself."

"Never mind how I heard. I want to know if the report is true." And Howard Griselda, lighting his pipe, puffed and watched Joe carefully through the smoke.

"Well, it's not quite true. My mother will be in command of the place. I won't have much to do with the operation except getting it started. Why do you ask?"

"Frankly, Sheriff, I don't think it appropriate for the chief law enforcement officer of the county to be operating a place with such a shady reputation."

Blue-gray wisps and curls of smoke drifted between the two men. Joe asked, "Can I talk to you man-to-man, off the record?"

"No, Sheriff, I don't think so. Better figure that I'm here as a representative of the paper."

"Well, I'll talk to you anyway. Fact is, the past reputation of the place cuts no ice. My mother will be in charge, and I don't think that she'll put up with anything crude. The reputation of the place would simply have to change. As far as my being Sheriff, I'm also human. I realize I'm in an exposed position, especially with you guarding my reputation the way you do. Just the same I think I should be allowed to invest my money in any legal way I see fit without a lot of breastbeating and innuendo in the newspapers. That's just plain justice."

Griselda nodded his massive head. "I agree, to a certain extent. But don't forget that as sheriff, you're like Caesar's wife. Running a roadhouse seems, well, tactless and inadvisable. It's just not in good taste."

"Come now, Howard. This isn't 1890. Just because a place has a bar doesn't make it disreputable. Halfway House is a quaint old country hotel, or it will be if I take over. The place has been on the market for months now, and I can't see that I'm taking advantage of anybody buying it."

"You learned about it while engaged on public business."

"About eight o'clock one night. So what?"

Griselda heaved himself to his feet. "This may all be true; still I think the voters are entitled to know that the Sheriff is planning to open and operate a tavern."

Joe laughed nervously. "You make the deal sound like an act of moral decay."

"Those are your words, not mine."

Griselda took his leave. Joe sat brooding. Casey Miggs telephoned to report that Bill Whipple definitely could not be located.

"I'll see him tomorrow," said Joe. "Right now I'm tired and ill. I'm going home and wrap my head in a hot towel."

6

Joe sat on the living room couch, feet on the coffee table. Miranda, coming into the room, saw that something was amiss. She dropped beside him, took hold of his elbow. "What's the trouble, Daddy? Is it that Bill Whipple? You're not champion fighter of the world, so why worry?"

Joe roused himself. "Who says I'm not? Bill Whipple? I was just toying with him."

"Be serious, Daddy!"

Joe threw up his hands. "You come to jolly me up, and the first thing you say is 'be serious'."

Miranda tugged his arm in vexation. "I want to know what's worrying you."

"It's no secret. It sure won't be after Monday's paper. Howard Griselda doesn't approve of Halfway House."

"How silly!"

"I know it's silly. You know it's silly. Howard Griselda thinks it's news. I can't figure how he got wind of the deal so fast. The real estate agent wouldn't talk. Nobody else knew."

Miranda suddenly became indignant. "It's that gossipy Gwen Griselda. Everything she hears she blabs to her father!"

"Aha!" said Joe. "The light dawns. You told Gwen Griselda, eh?"

"Well, we were talking about the summer and what we were doing, and I mentioned Halfway House. I don't see why she has to be so garrulous."

"She probably didn't have a chance to say a word. What other family secrets did you disclose?"

"I didn't know this was a family secret."

"Well, it isn't. Except now Howard Griselda can make me look like a crook."

"That's ridiculous! It's not that we're doing anything wrong! Can't you get back at him some way?"

Joe gave a sour grunt. "First of all I don't own a newspaper. Secondly, even if I did, he hasn't done anything off color I could write up. Howard is the kind of guy that pasteurizes his own milk."

Miranda frowned reflectively. "I hear a lot from Gwen about her father — just as much as she hears from me."

"Oh? What's Howard Griselda been doing that I can put him in jail for, on the testimony of his daughter?"

"Let me think..."

7

On Monday morning Joe telephoned the editorial offices of the *Pleasant Grove Messenger*. "Howard, are you planning to run that piece about me today?"

"I sure am, Sheriff. Nothing personal, you understand. A newspaper is the watch-dog of the community. Whatever the voters should know I tell them."

"All well and good. But it's only fair that you run a little piece signed by me, explaining my side of the situation. The voters also have a right to that information."

"Very well," said Griselda ponderously. "I'll do that. When can you get your statement over here?"

"In about an hour."

Joe wrote:

> So far as I can see, Mr. Griselda makes two complaints
> about my investing money in real estate. First: Halfway

House has had a shady reputation over the years. I told Mr. Griselda that he has a legitimate complaint if the reputation continues bad after my blameless old mother runs it a year or two. Second: he charges that I came upon the opportunity in the course of my professional duties. In a certain far-fetched sense this is true. What of it? Such is more or less standard practice for everyone. For instance, Mr. Griselda, editor and publisher of the *Messenger*, carefully studies all classified advertising before it is printed. Items he needs for his own household or bargains he knows he can sell at a quick profit he deals for before the newspaper is on the stands.

This, of course, is not illegal, nor even in the strictest sense dishonest, even though, during the last year or so, Mr. Griselda has bought from advertisers — before the public had a chance to see the advertisement — the following:

- 2 automobiles, at extreme sacrifice prices, from a boy inducted into the army, and from a widow who needed money desperately.
- A near-new power lawn-mower for $10.
- A new lawn swing for $7.50.
- An exercise machine, a bathtub whirlpool massager and a sunlamp for $40.
- A stamp collection he values at $700 for $50.
- A fur coat for his wife for $32.

In addition he collects the regular fee for running the advertisement.

I mention these matters not because I believe Mr. Griselda to be a crook, or hardly even a hypocrite, but merely a man who is more conscious of other people's failings than his own.

Joe sent the statement to the *Messenger* office. There was no acknowl-edgment from Howard Griselda. The statement did not appear in the afternoon paper, but neither did the editorial impugning Joe's purchase of Halfway House.

8

Joe drove out Madrone Way to Mrs. Bazzarini's house. The day was bright, the sunlight a glare tempered by cold air drifting over the mountains from the Pacific. Murder, killing, anger were completely incongruous to the surroundings. The golf course spread green and tranquil; Spanish Hill loomed high, a darker green veined with brown and tan, dappled with black shadow. It would be nice to live out here on Madrone Way, thought Joe — provided of course that he broke the Mooney case and could feel confident that his neighbors were not murderers.

Mrs. Bazzarini greeted him with affability, and asked Miss Locke to bring Joe a cup of coffee or a glass of wine, whichever was to Joe's taste.

Joe requested coffee, and Miss Locke left the room. Mrs. Bazzarini inquired as to the progress of the case.

"To tell the truth," said Joe, "I'm not much nearer now than I was Tuesday morning, although I've narrowed the field down. Incidentally, I'd like to ask you a very personal question."

Here Miss Locke entered the room with the coffee. She put the cup on a table convenient to Joe, then plumped Mrs. Bazzarini's pillows, adjusted the curtain and prepared to take a seat. "Excuse me, Miss Locke," said Joe. "If you don't mind, I'd like to talk privately with Mrs. Bazzarini."

With a snort Miss Locke withdrew.

"I imagine that you are a wealthy woman," said Joe.

"Yes, I would say so. Not that the money does me any good."

"What I want to ask is this: who inherits upon your death?"

Mrs. Bazzarini gave an uneasy grimace, not liking the sound of the word 'death'. "Well, this is something I had planned never to talk about, because now it is impossible."

"I won't tell a soul," said Joe. "Unless it becomes absolutely necessary."

"Well, I had written a new will leaving a large sum to Ken. He was such a sweet boy and he treated me so much nicer than my own flesh and blood. Do you think Laura ever comes to see me? And that fat donkey of a husband? Never. They're too good for me." Mrs. Bazzarini's round face became pink with spite. "I wrote a will giving Laura ten thousand and I left the rest to Ken: a very large amount of property. I know he would have enjoyed it and gotten good use from it and maybe thought of old Mrs. Bazzarini once in a while."

"Yes, I'm sure he would have done so," said Joe. "Er — what did Laura and her husband think about this?"

"I don't think they believed me."

"You told them?"

"I said something to the effect that I wanted to do nice things for people that were nice to me, and that people who took things for granted were going to get a shock when I died."

"What did Mr. and Mrs. Hubman say as to this?"

"They just laughed. They thought I was fooling."

"Now who gets your money?"

"I haven't made up my mind. Caspar and Laura, I suppose. She is my daughter, though she hardly acts like one."

Joe sipped the coffee and wondered if Miss Locke were eavesdropping. Well, it didn't make much difference. The main thing was the information. For the first time, a motive for the death of Ken had emerged from the welter. The idea of portly Caspar in Ken's uniform was grotesque. Laura Hubman? Strange, but not grotesque. Possible, but hardly probable. The same with everyone else along Madrone Way. And who was the woman who had phoned the tip to Howard Griselda? More likely Miss Locke.

Joe asked, "Did Ken know that you planned to remember him in your will?"

Mrs. Bazzarini colored, and looked away. "Well, I gave him to understand that he wouldn't be forgotten. It embarrassed him. He was such a simple nice boy, the thought that somebody wanted to do something embarrassed him."

Joe took his leave. He stopped by the Whipple house, and found Sheila Whipple at home. Joe asked the whereabouts of Bill, and Sheila professed ignorance. "I don't know where he is. He's not at work; I was just talking to Fred and Fred hadn't seen him. In fact he didn't come home last night at all."

"Is that right now," said Joe thoughtfully. "You saw him when?"

"It was late yesterday afternoon. He was in one of his moods, and when he's like that nobody can talk to him. I just never try. He went out in the evening, and stayed out all night."

"You don't have any idea where he stayed?"

"No sir, I do not. It couldn't have been far, because he didn't take his car. It's not like him. To tell you the truth I'm worried. He wasn't dressed to go out. I called one or two of his friends, but no one has seen him."

"No one came to pick him up?"

"I couldn't say for sure. He was very moody, walking back and forth. Then he went out the door and that's the last we saw of him."

"Hmm. Does he do that often?"

"He's just unpredictable. I've never been able to figure him out, even when he was a little boy. I don't envy the girl that marries him. I didn't start to worry until just an hour or so ago."

"If he comes in, please tell him I want to talk to him. In fact, have him give me a call."

Mrs. Whipple nodded. "I hope he's all right...He wouldn't go anywhere without taking his car."

9

An hour later, at about eleven o'clock, Bill Whipple's body was discovered by Mrs. Bazzarini's gardener, to the side of her tool shed. Dr. Hesketh, the coroner, was of the opinion that Bill Whipple had been killed with an instrument similar or identical to that which had killed Ken Mooney — probably an ordinary carpenter's hammer.

Chapter X

1

THE BODY LAY SPRAWLED and rigid, arms and legs up, like a dog lying on its back. Sickening, thought Joe, how murder plundered a man of his dignity. He thought of Bill Whipple in the bar at Halfway House: quick, strong, furious. And look at him now. If it hadn't been for the gardener going behind the shed to urinate, the body might have remained undiscovered for days.

There were wheel tracks in the soil, and Joe deduced a wheelbarrow. Late last night Madrone Way must have witnessed a macabre scene. After midnight the street would be empty and everyone asleep, with no one to notice the dark figure trundling a wheelbarrow from which protruded arms and legs.

One thing was clear: Bill Whipple could be excused from his role as suspect in the killing of Ken Mooney. "Rex," said Joe, "go along Madrone Way and check every wheelbarrow."

Rex Kelly departed on his mission.

Joe made a plaster cast of the wheel tracks. Photographs had already been made. The body was removed, with Mrs. Bazzarini's blank white face peering from the window.

Joe went into the Bazzarini house, but Miss Locke advised against talking to Mrs. Bazzarini. "She'll become hysterical at a single word. And I don't dare sedate her."

"She didn't hear anything last night?"

"No sir. She did not."

"Could you get me the night nurse's telephone number?"

"Yes. It's Mrs. Warringer." She wrote the number for Joe. He telephoned, made contact with Mrs. Warringer, who stated that she had heard nothing the previous night.

Joe returned to the street, where he met Rex Kelly. "I've located the wheelbarrow," said Kelly. "In front of the Benjamin house."

"What did you find?" asked Joe.

"Blood and fiber. Matter of fact, I remembered seeing the wheelbarrow. I checked it out first, and hit the jackpot. Just like that."

"I guess we better go talk to Mrs. Benjamin, which is a drag." Grace Benjamin did not invite them into the house, but came out to stand on the porch. Joe indicated the wheelbarrow on a gravel walkway which ran across the front of the house, above the slope of her new lawn.

"I guess you've heard the news," said Joe.

"No, I'm afraid not," said Mrs. Benjamin. "What is the news?"

"Bill Whipple was murdered last night."

Grace Benjamin's face changed little, except possibly to become more severe. "Do you know who did it?"

"Quite likely the same person who killed Ken Mooney, and it seems that the murderer took your wheelbarrow to move the corpse."

"What?" Grace Benjamin showed far more outrage at the news that her wheelbarrow had been used than at the announcement of Bill Whipple's death.

"That's what it looks like," said Joe. "We find traces of blood and wisps of fiber corresponding to Bill Whipple's clothes, and the dirt on his clothes seems to match the dirt in the wheelbarrow."

"Please don't blame me," said Mrs. Benjamin in her iciest voice. "I'm afraid I have no alibi, as I believe it's called."

"No, no," said Joe, "we're not accusing anybody; we just want to know if you heard the wheelbarrow being used, or any disturbance whatever."

"No, I'm sorry," said Mrs. Benjamin, somewhat mollified. "I heard nothing."

"How long has the wheelbarrow been where it is now?"

"Since last Thursday. The gardener used it to mulch the lawn, then neglected to take it in the back. I don't care to do it myself, naturally. Are you going to take away the wheelbarrow?"

"I suppose we'd better."

"Please be careful of my lawn."

Joe and Rex Kelly retreated to the street.

Joe stood rubbing his chin. "Well, I guess I'll hand you some more legwork. The usual, up and down the street. Alibis, if feasible. Who everybody was sleeping with and how long. Did they hear any noise? Did they see Bill Whipple last night? Any ideas why he might have been killed, and so on."

"What about the wheelbarrow?"

"I don't know. I suppose we should take it in, although I don't know what we can prove by it."

Sally Wagner came out from her house, wearing a purple and red housecoat. "Has something happened? I saw the ambulance go by."

"We've had another killing," said Joe.

"Oh my!" Sally Wagner stood with fists clenched. "Who?"

"Bill Whipple."

"And you still don't know who's responsible?"

"Not yet."

"But this is terrifying! It's as if a madman were loose!"

"I hardly think it's a madman. Ken and Bill were killed for a sufficient reason. The reason of course may be mad."

"But how can a person feel safe?" cried Sally Wagner, darting glances right and left.

"Well, I hope to have the murderer put away before too long," said Joe. He turned to Rex Kelly. "Better take the wheelbarrow into the lab, Rex. If we don't, it'll turn out to be an indispensable clue."

Rex Kelly started up the slope toward the wheelbarrow. Instantly a window swung open and Mrs. Benjamin called: "Will you *please* not walk over the freshly seeded lawn?"

"Sorry, ma'am." Rex Kelly jumped back to the street and approached the wheelbarrow by a roundabout route. Mrs. Benjamin, after a brief look at Mrs. Wagner, closed the window. Mrs. Wagner pointedly turned her back, and watched Rex Kelly gingerly rolling the wheelbarrow along Mrs. Benjamin's gravel walk.

"The murderer avoided a grisly fate," Joe pointed out. "He took pains not to trample Mrs. Benjamin's lawn."

Sally Wagner emitted a raucous hoot of laughter, which she quickly stifled. "I don't know why I'm laughing — because really I'm frightened. I don't think I'll stir out of my house or see anyone until this terrible business is over with."

"You don't have friends who would come stay with you?"

"And have them get killed? They wouldn't thank me…I might go visit my sister in Santa Monica. On the other hand I might not. We can't take much of each other — too much alike, I guess. And now," Sally Wagner gave a sour chuckle, "I've been invited to the baby shower for Grace Benjamin at Ethel Taylor's today. But I'm darned if I'll be a hypocrite and go. Perhaps I should visit the Whipples. Poor unhappy people!"

"It's a dreadful business," said Joe, starting to detach himself. "Well, I—"

"I'm going to think very earnestly about this affair," said Sally Wagner. "I just might be able to see something that everyone else has missed."

"Tell me first if you do," said Joe. He went up Madrone Way toward the Whipple house. Sally Wagner remained on the sidewalk, staring at the wheelbarrow in an attitude of cogitation, staring so intently indeed that Joe, turning into the Whipple driveway, paused to watch her. And Sally Wagner looked from the wheelbarrow to the new-seeded lawn, scanning the surface carefully, as if seeking footprints — an operation Joe had already conducted, without success. Sally Wagner, however, seemed not at all disconcerted by the lack, and only stared more intently than ever. "If she's got a theory, it's more than I've got," Joe told himself. Sally Wagner abruptly turned and walked swiftly into her own house. Joe pressed the Whipples' front door bell. Fred Whipple responded, face thin and white. "Sorry to intrude upon you, Mr. Whipple," said Joe.

Fred Whipple gave his head a shake. "It's no intrusion. I'm glad to see you. I want to help you as much as I can."

Fred Whipple was not so tall nor so spare nor so aquiline as his son, and his mannerisms were less abrupt; still there was no mistaking the resemblance.

Joe entered the house. Fred Whipple did not ask him to sit, and the two men stood in a red-tiled foyer off the living room.

"I suspect — I can't be sure — that whoever killed Ken Mooney killed Bill," said Joe. "Can you think of any reason why this should be so?"

"No. I certainly can't. The thing seems — impossible. I can't understand why it should happen."

Joe asked further questions regarding Bill, his work at Whipple Chevrolet, his plans and prospects, but learned nothing important. "Bill was a hard worker," said Fred, "with enormous drive and ambition. Once he took hold of something he never let it drop. A lot of people didn't like him, but they all respected him."

"How did he get on with people up and down Madrone Way?"

Fred's thin mouth twisted. "About as you'd expect. We've never been accepted and we've lived here almost eight years. Well, that's not quite true. The Taylors are real fine people; in fact they invited Sheila to some kind of affair today. Naturally she's not going. We've hit it off fairly well with Mrs. Wagner, but the Shortridges, the Hubmans, the Gentrys, the Mortimers, the Benjamins — they're all too good for us."

"How did Marsh Shortridge and Bill get along?"

"Hated each other. They had a run-in years ago when Bill built a shack up on the hill — or was it Starr? I forget the details. Anyway they've never been friendly."

"I'd like to look through Bill's personal gear," said Joe. "It's just possible there's something which might give us a lead."

Fred Whipple shrugged. "Up the stairs, first door to the right. Please be quiet. Sheila's had a sedative, but I don't think she's asleep. This is the worst thing which has ever happened to us..."

Bill's room was neat and somewhat characterless. There were a bed, a chest of drawers, a desk, a book-case containing college texts, a collection of model airplanes, football trophies, a stack of *Mad* and *Playboy* magazines. The walls displayed what appeared to be Bill's main field of interest: girls. Photographs of all sizes, girls of all descriptions, snapshots, signed portraits, enlargements. Joe recognized none of them. They seemed to represent Bill's career at San Jose State.

Joe went through Bill's desk. There was a Polaroid camera, a shoebox full of prints, again mostly girls, and some of these pictures caused Joe to lift his eyebrows.

In a closet hung Bill's wardrobe: four or five suits, a half-dozen jackets with matching slacks, numerous sportshirts. Joe, who owned a single dark blue suit, decided that Bill was something of a clotheshorse.

Joe rummaged through pockets, found nothing more significant than a package of prophylactics.

On the chest lay Bill's wallet, where he had flung it the night before. Within was the usual collection of credit cards and business cards, thirty-two dollars, memoranda and receipts. One of these latter aroused Joe's notice: a numbered call-slip at Hobbs Camera Shop on Main Street, dated the day previously. Joe tucked the slip into his own wallet.

He left the room and walked downstairs. Fred Whipple, sitting in the living room, rose slowly to his feet. "Well, Sheriff, what do you think?"

"Frankly, Mr. Whipple, I'm mystified."

2

Joe drove down Main Street, parked in front of the Hobbs Camera Shop and went in. Behind the counter stood Mrs. Hobbs, who failed to recognize him. "Yes sir?"

"Is Mr. Hobbs in?"

"I'll call him. Who shall I say?"

Hobbs appeared, wearing a gray laboratory smock: a sallow old-looking man of forty with a ragged ginger crew-cut. Joe brought out the claim check. "I'm Sheriff Bain, Mr. Hobbs. Official business."

An expression of vague apprehension crossed Hobbs' face. "Something connected with the shop?"

"Indirectly. Yesterday a young man named Bill Whipple brought some work in here for you and you gave him this claim check."

Hobbs examined the check. "Bill Whipple? Yes, I know him. He had a kind of a special job." Hobbs hesitated. "I don't know whether I should talk about it or not without his being here. After all, it's his business—"

"Bill Whipple is dead," said Joe. "Homicide. I'm investigating the case."

"Oh! It's hard to believe! Why, I was just talking to him last night!"

"I know. Did he have anything much to say?"

"Just in regard to what he wanted me to do, which was make enlargements from a Polaroid print."

"Do you have the print?"

"No. He didn't want to leave it. I took it into the darkroom, copied it — that is, I made the negative — and gave it back to him. In fact, I was just printing the enlargements when you came in."

"Can I see them?"

"Sure thing. They're wet, but that don't matter. But what happened to Bill Whipple?"

"He got hit over the head with a hammer."

Hobbs disappeared into the rear premises. A minute later he came out holding an 8 × 10 enlargement, still wet and limp. "It's a bit fuzzy," said Hobbs apologetically. "Every time you process a picture you degrade the image by maybe ten percent, no matter how good your equipment. I made a negative, that's one process, I printed the negative, that's the second, so this is only about eighty percent as sharp as the original."

"Yeah," said Joe. "Let's see the picture."

Hobbs laid it down on the counter. The picture had been taken in the bar at Halfway House, with the camera pointed into the mirror, to record the image of four people sitting at the bar. They were Ken Mooney, Bill Whipple, who held the camera, Alice Benjamin and another girl with a great vulgar bush of dark hair. On the bar, somewhat to the side, was a miniature Christmas tree.

Joe asked, "Where is the negative?"

"In the darkroom."

"I better take it with me."

Hobbs grimaced sadly for the departure of the $7.50 he had been planning to charge Bill Whipple. He went into the darkroom, to return with an envelope and a sour face which Joe assessed as the loss of at least two votes next election.

"If you're out any money," said Joe, "bill Fred Whipple on Madrone Way. I'll mention the situation to him, and I don't think there'll be any problem."

"Thanks very much, Sheriff," said Hobbs, his face magically transformed. "I'll just do that."

Joe walked slowly to his car. The picture — an eery record from the past, when all was different, when Ken and Bill were alive, when no one had dreamed of murder.

Who was with whom? Joe examined the picture. The pairing was not clear. It might be either way.

Joe drove back up Madrone Way, parked in front of Mrs. Benjamin's house. He walked up the steps, pressed the button.

There was a wait. Joe rang again, and then the door opened. Mrs. Benjamin, very pregnant in a dressing gown, her face damp, her hair tied up in a pony tail, looked out the door. "Yes, Sheriff?"

"May I come in a minute? I have a question or two."

Mrs. Benjamin ungraciously allowed him to enter. "It's almost half-past two. I'm due at Mrs. Taylor's and I haven't even started to dress."

"I won't be long," said Joe. "You remember that I asked you if Alice had ever been friendly with Ken Mooney."

"Yes, I remember you asked," said Mrs. Benjamin. "I believe I stated that they probably had known each other at high school."

"What about Bill Whipple?"

"Naturally they were acquainted."

"Was there ever any romantic attachment?"

Mrs. Benjamin gave a faint snort of disgust. "I should hardly think so — not with Bill Whipple's reputation."

"Did Alice go out with either Ken or Bill last Christmas?"

"Of course not! Alice is engaged to Marsh Shortridge. She is very much in love."

"She was engaged last Christmas?"

"Certainly."

"What do you make of this?" Joe handed Mrs. Benjamin the photograph.

"Hm…hm…" Grace Benjamin frowned, suddenly no longer either serene or impatient. "Where was this taken?"

"At Halfway House, a bar that Ken owned."

"I must say I'm surprised. Yes, surprised. In fact, I'm — well…" Her voice trailed off. She examined the photograph again, then looked up. "Has Marsh Shortridge seen this picture?"

"I hardly think so."

Mrs. Benjamin essayed an ingratiating smile. "I suggest, I hope, that you won't show it to him. He'd be very upset. The circumstances I'm sure were innocent, but I doubt if Marsh would understand." And

Grace Benjamin's smile, which she tried to make soft and persuasive, was curiously affecting. "In fact — may I keep the photograph?"

"I'm afraid not, Mrs. Benjamin. Both these boys are dead. When will Alice be home?"

"Toward the end of the summer. There's no definite date."

"How could I get in touch with her?"

"There's no very convenient way. You could write her care of American Express, Paris. I imagine that she'll be in to pick up her mail in the near future."

Grace Benjamin went to the mantle, returned with a card postmarked a week or two previously at Bilbao, Spain. "That's the last card I've had from her," said Mrs. Benjamin. "She doesn't write very frequently."

"If I may ask a personal question — where did she get the money to travel?"

Grace Benjamin took the question evenly. "From her father. He doesn't approve of the marriage and I think he hoped that Alice might change her mind."

"And what do you think?"

"If she doesn't want to marry Marsh, she might as well find out sooner as later. Marriage is a permanent contract."

Joe re-read the postcard. Alice was well, enjoying herself and planned to be returning shortly to Paris. Joe glumly returned the card. Superficially, all was in order; Alice was in Europe and remote from the Pleasant Grove murders. On the other hand, jets flew daily between Paris and San Francisco.

Mrs. Benjamin began to make restless motions. "If you'll excuse me, Sheriff, I think I had better get dressed, or I'll be late for the shower — which after all is in my honor."

"When do you expect your husband home, Mrs. Benjamin?"

"As to that, I'm not quite sure. Why don't you write him and ask?"

"I'll probably do that." Joe departed the Benjamin house. He stood on the sidewalk a discomfited moment or two, then jumped into his car and drove to Shortridge's Department Store.

Marsh Shortridge was not in his office. The receptionist looked twice to make sure. "He was here a few minutes ago. I know he'll be back because there's a sales conference scheduled for three."

"I'll wait," said Joe. He went into Marsh's office, where he examined a studio portrait of Alice on Marsh's desk: a winsome face, lacking Grace Benjamin's grimness. Married to Marsh, this might come in the course of the years, thought Joe. On the other hand, the marriage might be a glorious success. "Each has what the other wants," thought Joe. "Maybe that's how it should be." And he recalled his own raggle-taggle marriage.

Marsh Shortridge came into his office. He paused at the sight of Joe, then came forward, his round pale face void of expression. "What can I do for you, Sheriff?"

"Just a few questions, Mr. Shortridge. You know, I suppose, that Bill Whipple was killed last night?"

"So I've been informed."

"Do you have any ideas in regard to the situation?"

"I'm afraid I don't. Nothing very illuminating at any rate. I imagine that Bill and Ken Mooney got involved with some rough people."

"That's about what I figure too," said Joe. "The closest I can get to those rough people is that they live on Madrone Way. Incidentally, are you acquainted with any of Ken Mooney's girl friends?"

Marsh allowed an incredulous smile to cross his face. "I hardly think so."

"Have you ever visited Halfway House?"

"I've driven past. I've never stopped. It's a rather untidy old place."

"Did you know that Ken owned Halfway House?"

Marsh frowned. "I vaguely recall someone making a remark to this effect, but I didn't pay any great attention."

Joe picked up Alice's photograph. Marsh made a small motion, as if he wanted to take it from Joe's hands. "A beautiful girl," said Joe. "When is the marriage?"

"Early this fall."

"Where will you live?"

"We haven't decided definitely. I'd like to build a house up on top Spanish Hill, and I think that's what we'll do."

"That should be fine. You'd have a wonderful view, out over the valley."

Marsh gave a short nod.

"Incidentally, did you talk to Bill Whipple last night?"

"I did not."

"Hm, that's odd. I guess my informant was mistaken."

Marsh made no comment.

Joe controlled his exasperation, departed. Marsh was a cold fish. Joe wondered if Alice's Catholicism and her views toward marriage were as strong as those of her mother. She couldn't be too wild about Marsh Shortridge, what with Christmas parties and long engagements and gadding about Europe.

Joe went for a drive in the country to clear his mind, and was somewhat surprised to find himself pulling into the Pandora Realty driveway.

Luna prepared tea, which Joe accepted gingerly.

Luna listened attentively while Joe analyzed the case. "In theory, anybody along Madrone Way could have killed Bill Whipple. It was just a case of meeting him somewhere, then a whack with the hammer, and hiding him until late at night. That's the theory. In practice, Mrs. Bazzarini is out. The Whipples are out. If we assume the same person killed both Ken and Bill, the Taylors are just about out. The extra-pregnant Grace Benjamin is just about out. Sam and Miriam Shortridge are too unbelievable, and besides they had alibis for Ken's death. Caspar Hubman? Laura Hubman? Marsh Shortridge? Starr Shortridge? Sally Wagner? Which reminds me, I want to talk to Sally Wagner tonight. I'd swear that she had some kind of illumination."

"Telephone her, if you like," Luna suggested.

Joe checked the number, dialled, but received no answer. "Ten to one she's gone to stay in a motel," said Joe. "And I can't say as I blame her... I wonder what she saw that I didn't. She was looking at the wheelbarrow and the lawn."

He telephoned headquarters and spoke to Rex Kelly. "I don't have much," said Kelly. "A couple of iron-clad alibis."

"That's better than none. Who?"

"Sam and Miriam Shortridge were out to dinner, at the residence of Dr. and Mrs. Luther Norman; Tom and Ethel Taylor and all their kids were driving home from picnicking on Genesee Slough. Aside from this: nothing. Blanks."

"About what I feared," said Joe. "Well, if anything comes up call me at this number. I'll be here another hour or so."

Joe hung up. "What a mess."

"Will you have more tea?" asked Luna.

"Well — just about two fingers. Come over here and tell me about Arthemisia, and get my mind off my troubles."

"All three at once?" asked Luna demurely.

She poured the tea, which stimulated Joe's mental processes.

Presently the telephone rang. Luna answered. "Pandora Realty... It's for you, Joe."

"What now?" sighed Joe. "Joe Bain speaking."

"Ace Wardell here, Sheriff. There's a homicide on Madrone Way: Mrs. Sally Wagner."

"With a hammer, no doubt."

"With a hammer."

Chapter XI

1

Sally Wagner had disdained to attend Grace Benjamin's baby shower. She had locked herself in her house, concentrated on catching up with her domestic duties. She washed dishes, changed the bed-linen, vacuumed rugs, burnt rubbish in the back-yard incinerator. About three o'clock she went to the telephone, either to make a call or to answer one. While she sat talking, someone came up behind her, struck her with a hammer, then hung up the receiver. Through oversight, haste, or hysteria, the hammer had been forgotten and remained on the gray-violet rug under the telephone table: an ugly little tool with curved claws, one broken off near the tip, and a make-shift handle.

Investigating the scene of the crime, Joe traced Sally Wagner's activities. The dishes had been stacked to dry but not put away. The vacuum cleaner had been wheeled into the hall, possibly for use elsewhere. The trash baskets were yet outside by the incinerator, not all of their contents burned. There was no sign of forcible ingress; either the front or the back door had been unlocked. Or had Sally Wagner admitted the murderer of her own free will? Feather-brained woman, thought Joe.

The afternoon had been overcast; Sally Wagner had turned on the lights in her living room. As soon as dusk arrived, Grace Benjamin, looking from her bedroom down across fence and hedge, had seen the sprawled body through one of the picture windows.

The ambulance backed up the driveway, watched by residents, curiosity seekers, reporters from as far away as San Jose. Joe and Rex Kelly went out on the front porch to catch a breath of air.

"What gets me," said Joe peevishly, "is *why*? Did she figure out what was going on, who was responsible? If so, would she be idiotic enough to make the fact known?"

"Idiotic or not," said Rex Kelly glumly, "if she had any notion at all, she's smarter than I am."

"Well, we have the murder weapon, which is our first break. Here's another matter: who was Sally talking to when she got whacked? You better go find her personal phone book. Call all her friends, find out who she talked to today around three o'clock."

"Right." Rex Kelly went back into the house.

Tom Taylor approached Joe. "What's it look like, Sheriff?"

Joe, choosing among the responses which came to his mind, said, "We're following down every lead we can think of."

"How did the murderer get in?"

"At a guess, through the back door," said Joe. "I don't imagine the killer would dare use the front door."

"That's also a risk, with the Benjamin house overlooking the back yard."

"True, unless Grace Benjamin is guilty. And since I can't imagine her leaping that seven-foot fence in her current condition it must be somebody else. Hence, the murder occurred after Grace Benjamin left for the shower, when there wouldn't be any risk."

"Poor Sally Wagner," said Tom Taylor. "She was a good-hearted soul, although she made a lot of enemies with her voice. If she'd stayed on good terms with Grace Benjamin and gone to the shower, she'd be alive right now."

Another voice, gruff and sardonic, the voice of Howard Griselda, spoke: "She'd also be alive if the murderer had been apprehended. What about it, Sheriff?"

"Don't worry," declared Joe energetically, "I'll get him."

"Possibly by the process of elimination, when he and you are the only two persons in town left alive."

From the onlookers came chuckles and titters.

Joe grunted and went off to search the back yard.

2

On the following morning *Life* was again delivered to subscribers along that route which formerly had been serviced by Ken Mooney. The addresses of these magazines were listed, checked against the list which had been prepared from the previous week's distribution. No discrepancy was found, a fact which caused Joe to hold his head. "As if I didn't have enough on my mind. Now it's a case of an extra magazine!"

"Is it so important?" inquired Casey Miggs, who had assisted in the comparison of lists.

"Whatever can't be explained has got to be important. Where did the extra magazine come from?"

"Your guess is as good as mine," shrugged Miggs.

Joe made no reply. He went to the laboratory, tucked the murder weapon into a cellophane envelope, drove to Madrone Way, where he carried the hammer from house to house asking questions. To Joe's great surprise, Fred Whipple identified the hammer, declaring it to be a tool which he had inherited from his father — almost an heirloom. Seven or eight years previously Bill had lost the hammer while building a tree-house.

"And where was this tree-house?"

"Up on Spanish Hill. The Shortridge kids found it and pulled it down." Fred Whipple looked off through the smoke of his cigarette, seeing an immeasurable distance. "They just couldn't tolerate someone getting enjoyment out of their land. Bill wasn't doing a thing wrong. They chased him out like he was a bill collector. He always carried a grudge on account of that old tree-house and I guess I have too. Oh well. It's all in the past. Things are so different now. I think we'll sell out and go back to Oregon…"

Starr Shortridge remembered Bill Whipple's tree-house clearly. She spoke in a voice of studied coolness behind which Joe detected both anger and bewilderment. "I could show you the exact tree if you were interested. He made a dreadful mess — scraps of lumber, paper bags, orange peels. It was as if he had decided to lay claim to that part of Spanish Hill."

"What of the hammer?"

"I don't remember it. I mean I don't remember what it looked like. I know it was there — a hammer and a saw."

"What happened to the tools?"

"I don't know. I never thought of them again."

Joe spoke to Marsh at his office in the department store. He seemed more starchy and condescending than ever. Joe contained his irritation with an effort. Marsh wore an urbane black suit with a white shirt, a striped tie; he flicked a glance up and down Joe's whipcord trousers and dark brown poplin jacket as if he found them hard to believe.

"You remember Bill Whipple's tree-house?"

"Certainly. It was in an oak tree at the north end of our property. As soon as Starr and Alice called my attention to it, I went up and destroyed it."

"What did Bill Whipple say to this?"

"Nothing. He wasn't there."

"He had left his tools?"

"I believe so."

"What became of them?"

"I don't know."

"Did you return later to the site of the tree-house?"

"Oh yes. Sometime later, to clean up the rubbish. So far as I could see there had been no further trespass. The tools were gone." Marsh began to manipulate objects on his desk, as if he had urgent matters to which he must attend.

Joe said politely, "I won't take too much more of your time. Have you heard from Alice?"

"Not in the last week or so."

"She'll be on her way home pretty soon?"

"I believe so."

"A shame you couldn't have been married and gone to Europe on your honeymoon."

Marsh drummed the surface of his desk with his finger tips. "I've already been to Europe. Twice, as a matter of fact."

"So you considered it a good idea that Alice should go?"

"Naturally. She's having a wonderful time."

3

The death of Sally Wagner, like that of Ken Mooney and Bill Whipple, posed many puzzles. From the evidence of the half-empty wastebaskets it would seem that Sally Wagner had been burning rubbish immediately prior to her death. Joe theorized that her work had been interrupted by the phone call. Hearing the bell she had run into the house without locking the door, allowing the murderer an easy ingress. But what a fortuitous circumstance! And how dared the murderer attack while Sally Wagner was talking on the telephone? If she chanced to look up, to scream, to call out a name, the murderer's goose was cooked.

Rex Kelly had interrogated all of Sally Wagner's friends; he had called all the numbers listed in her private phone book, all the tradespeople with whom Sally Wagner did business — to no avail. No one admitted talking to Sally Wagner at the time of her death. A long distance call? A wrong number?

Henrietta Freycinet, head librarian at the county library and Sally Wagner's best friend, had telephoned about an hour before her death. According to Henrietta Freycinet, Sally Wagner had been strange and fey. "There was something on her mind. Definitely. It wasn't just normal excitement. Sally was an excitable woman, but this was perturbation. She said something about footprints on Mrs. Benjamin's lawn —"

"Footprints on Mrs. Benjamin's lawn? We didn't see any footprints."

"That's what she said. And then she said something like: 'I have a funny feeling, as if I'm dreaming. I see something and I can't believe it.' Naturally I asked her what she knew, but she wouldn't tell me. I was just a bit miffed, and I suppose I sounded it. I told her that if she knew anything she had better tell the police."

"And what did she say to that?"

"She was very vague and evasive."

Henrietta Freycinet had nothing more to offer, and Joe was left to grope among imponderables. Sally Wagner either had not known the identity of the murderer, or she had. In the first case, why was she killed? In the second case, why did she not immediately communicate her knowledge to the police?

Paradoxes, contradictions.

Days passed. From the photograph which Bill Whipple had taken from the bar at Halfway House Joe isolated and blew up the face of the dark-haired girl. He showed this face to the Mooney family, to the residents of Madrone Way, to the faculty at Pleasant Grove High School and Aurora High School. He found no one who recognized the girl.

Ennis Mooney, the older of Ken's sisters, thought that Ken had mentioned driving to Gilroy, in Santa Clara County. Extending his inquiries to Gilroy, Joe finally identified the girl. She was Helen Ferguson, a stenographer in the office of Gilroy Building Supply.

Helen Ferguson, when Joe finally spoke to her, was irritable and emotional. "I haven't done anything wrong, and I don't want to talk to you!"

"I didn't accuse you of anything," said Joe. "I just asked if you knew Ken Mooney."

"Who I know is my own business!" And Helen Ferguson, putting her face in her hands, began to weep noisily.

Joe exhibited the entire photograph. "There's Ken Mooney, there's Bill Whipple, there's Alice Benjamin. Both of these boys are dead. You say you still don't know them? Maybe I better talk to your father."

"No!" exclaimed Helen Ferguson. "Don't tell my father. And don't show him that picture!"

"Well then, who were you with: Ken or Bill?"

"Ken."

"Alice was with Bill?"

Helen nodded sullenly. "I didn't like either one of them. Bill was a big pain, thinking he was so good. Alice — well, she thought she was pretty good too. They deserved each other. I told Ken I'd never go out with them again. They acted like I was some kind of little country girl. Even Ken got mad about the way they acted."

"You'd never met Bill or Alice before?"

"I'd seen Bill before, when we fixed up the party. He was real nice then. But as soon as he got with Alice he changed."

"Changed? How?"

"Well, I can't hardly describe it. I was surprised to see a girl like Alice with him. She seemed so prissy and lady-like, as if she thought she shouldn't be there. For a fact she shouldn't have been. Because once she took a drink she really discarded her inhibitions. I guess I did too. That's all the boys have in their minds: to take a girl somewhere and try to get her to drink."

"They succeeded, eh?"

"Yes," said Helen ruefully. "They succeeded. Oh how they succeeded. They had champagne. I love champagne."

"I assume then that things got a little out of hand."

"Yes, they did." Her lips curved in a vague retrospective smile.

"You split up and went to the bedrooms?"

"I don't want to say. If anything ever got back to my father —"

"I don't plan to say anything to him."

"Well then — yes, we did. I don't know about Bill and Alice, because Ken and I went first. It looked to me as if Alice was having second thoughts." Helen gave a little shudder. "It wouldn't have cut any ice with Bill. He was single-minded. He didn't even seem to be having fun! He came for one thing. I imagine he got it. Ken at least was considerate."

"Did you see Bill and Alice again?"

"No. I went out with Ken a few more times, until my father put a stop to it."

Joe took Helen backward and forward over the story. "Did Alice act like she was in love with Bill?"

"I don't know how she acted," said Helen irritably. "I didn't like her; she hardly talked to me."

Joe cautioned Helen against drinking champagne if she wanted to stay out of trouble and returned to Pleasant Grove. What had he learned? Alice Benjamin and Bill Whipple for reasons more or less complicated had gone to bed together during the previous Christmas holidays, although Alice had been engaged to Marsh at the time. Alice might not be too anxious to marry Marsh, thought Joe. She gained wealth, social position, a new house — but the bargain included Marsh Shortridge. No wonder she drank champagne and discarded inhibitions.

4

A week went by, then another, and another and another. Along Madrone Way there was no relaxation, and there never would be until the identity of the murderer was made known. If this never happened, then for all the years to come the folk would watch each other askance, knowing that among their number was someone who had killed three people.

Toward the end of August Joe happened to meet Ethel Taylor on Courthouse Avenue. "Have you heard the news?" she asked.

"If it's another murder, don't tell me," said Joe.

Ethel Taylor responded to the pleasantry with an uncertain smile. "It's rather more cheerful. Mrs. Benjamin has had her baby, a month early. She's named it Beatrice."

Joe made a congratulatory remark. "What else do you know that's new and interesting?"

"The Whipples have their house up for sale. Sally Wagner's house has gone to her sister, Mrs. Wanda Tobias. And wonder of wonders, I saw Mrs. Bazzarini taking a walk the other day. The old lady is actually improving."

Joe reflected a moment. "I still can't think of her as a suspect."

Ethel Taylor gave an uneasy laugh. "I suppose we've all had the same thoughts. But it couldn't be poor Mrs. Bazzarini. I know it wasn't Tom. He's the kindest man in the world. And it wasn't me, I assure you of that."

"It doesn't leave much of a list," said Joe. "Well, I must be off about my duties."

5

The *Pleasant Grove Messenger*, after a quizzical silence on the subject of the murders, gave Joe no respite. Every day a polite paragraph reported Sheriff Joe Bain in a state of bafflement, and occasionally there was speculation as to who might be the next victim, since murder in San Rodrigo County seemed so effortless: "A safe and convenient method of taking out your aggressions," wrote Howard Griselda. "While we do not recommend murder as a means of achieving mental health, still, if murder you must, San Rodrigo County appears as salubrious an environment as any."

For a period Griselda became distracted by the Secretary of Agriculture's *bracero* program. Not until the first week in September did he make a new reference to the murders. On September 10 he called upon Joe to make a forthright announcement as to whether or not he considered the crimes beyond his capacity to solve. "If so," wrote Howard Griselda, "it appears that appropriate assistance from Sacramento should be, or more properly, should have been, requested. Or does Sheriff Bain disdain expert assistance at the price of some new atrocity?"

The society page of the same edition announced the return of Alice Benjamin from Europe, and revealed that her marriage to Marshall Shortridge was to occur on September 21, less than two weeks away.

Already ruffled by Howard Griselda's editorial, Joe gave a growl of exasperation. "Why doesn't somebody let me in on things like this? Don't they know there's a murder investigation in progress?" He telephoned the Benjamin residence. Grace Benjamin responded.

"Sheriff Joe Bain, Mrs. Benjamin. I understand that Alice is home."

"Yes, she is." Grace Benjamin seemed less acerb than usual.

"I want to ask her a few questions. Is she home now?"

Mrs. Benjamin's voice became doubtful. "I think she's getting ready to go to Pebble Beach with Marsh."

"I'd better send a car out to pick her up," said Joe. "I want to talk with her."

"I'm sure she would prefer to talk with you here," said Mrs. Benjamin coldly.

"Very well," said Joe. "I'll be there in ten minutes or so."

Grace Benjamin met Joe at the door and grudgingly allowed him into the living room. "Alice is still tired from traveling. I hope you won't be too long."

"If she's so tired, why is she going to Pebble Beach? You don't seem to realize that this is a murder investigation. Everything else stops. It's like a big fire truck coming down the street. And why didn't you notify me that Alice was home?"

"If you must know," said Mrs. Benjamin frigidly, "I didn't want her harassed and molested."

"Your wants in a situation of this kind are unimportant, Mrs. Benjamin. Now if you'll please ask Alice to step in here."

Grace Benjamin walked to the stairs. "Alice? Will you please come down for a moment?"

Chapter XII

1

Joe had seen pictures of Alice, he had heard legends of her astounding beauty, but still his jaw dropped when she came into the room. She was perfect in every aspect: more than perfect, through indefinable graces and fascinating contradictions. She looked delicate but durable, youthful but knowing, slender and frail but supple and sure. She was an angelic being superior to the ordinary ruck; her substance, compared to human stuff, was like sugar to sand. Her style, compounded of artlessness, wistful charm, melancholy, was hers alone. No man's heart could fail to skip and flutter at the sight of her.

Joe heaved a sigh, introduced himself, looked pointedly at Mrs. Benjamin, who looked back. Finally Joe said, "I'd like to talk to Alice alone, if I may."

"I'd prefer to be present," said Mrs. Benjamin.

"Maybe you would. But when I ask her a question, I don't want her looking at you before she answers."

"She can answer without looking at me. But I wish to be present."

"Now look here, Mrs. Benjamin, let's get something straight. This is a murder case. Either you want to cooperate or you don't. If you don't, I'll have to stop being friendly."

Mrs. Benjamin's face took on a mulish set. She groped for words. Before she could speak, Joe asked, "You want her to tell me the truth, don't you?"

"Of course, but —"

"Are you afraid she won't tell me the truth?"

"No."

"Then why do you want to stay?"

Grace Benjamin turned on her heel and left the room.

"Let's go sit down over here," said Joe. Alice wordlessly obliged. She was wearing a smoke-colored cotton frock with a white collar, and Joe thought she looked good enough to eat. But she seemed ill at ease, almost frightened.

"Relax," said Joe. "I'm not as harsh as I sound. Your mother is the kind of woman that has to be dealt firmly with."

Alice smiled wanly. "She's pretty firm herself."

"You can be glad you don't take after her," said Joe. "Well, then. I guess you know what I want to talk about?"

Alice shook her head, and Joe again sensed apprehension.

"The murders of Ken Mooney, Bill Whipple and Sally Wagner — all friends of yours."

Alice nodded numbly.

"What do you think about these murders?"

"Just what everyone else thinks. They're awful."

"Have you any idea why they were killed?"

"No."

"You've been in Europe all summer?"

"Yes," said Alice hesitantly. Watching closely, Joe saw her shoulders droop.

"When did you get back?"

"A few days ago."

"Maybe I better take a look at your passport."

"Passport?"

"Yeah. The little blue book with your picture in it."

"I don't quite know where it is."

"When did you get back — exactly?"

Alice's face became doleful. She looked down at her hands, then looked across the room toward the door. Joe looked too, but Mrs. Benjamin was nowhere to be seen. Alice said in a husky voice, "I arrived in San Francisco about a month ago. On the first of August, to be exact. I'll show you the passport if you like. It's upstairs in my room."

"August first." A month and a half after Ken had been killed, something over a month after the deaths of Bill Whipple and Sally Wagner. "Where have you spent the last five weeks?"

Alice looked over her shoulder again, then shook her head miserably. "I don't want to tell you. I don't want anyone to know."

"Why not?"

"I just don't."

"Does your mother know?"

Alice shook her head.

"What about Marsh?"

Alice shook her head decidedly. "Definitely not."

"In other words — your mother knows."

Alice licked her lips. "I hope not."

"Well, you can tell me," said Joe. "I'll check up, and if there's no connection with the murder, no one will know."

Alice began to cry: quietly, with great restraint. Joe waited. Finally Alice said, "In a week I'm being married — to a very respectable young man. He's about as respectable as my mother."

Joe managed a crooked grin. "They'd make a good pair."

Alice went on in a dismal voice. "I'm not respectable at all. Frankly — if you must know — I'm marrying Marsh for his money. My mother approves of the marriage. I do too. I don't have anything against being secure. I don't want to be poor."

"What's wrong with being poor?" argued Joe. "I've been poor all my life."

"So have I," said Alice. "Don't judge us by the house."

"Well — what of that missing month?"

"I don't like to tell you."

"You were with a boy friend?"

Alice nodded, and again peered over her shoulder toward the door.

Joe cleared his throat. "If you want some unsolicited advice: don't marry the man. Marsh is as warm and enthusiastic as an oyster."

"I know... But he's — well, he's kind enough. And he's dependable."

"Life might be pretty uninteresting. Dependability and money aren't everything."

A hint of suppressed fury came into Alice's voice. "I'm doing it because I have to! We can't live otherwise! We're broke! Father isn't coming back from India. He's not sending any more money."

"What? That seems strange. Are you sure?"

"My mother says so."

"What of the baby — Beatrice? Doesn't he care about his offspring? He's responsible for child support."

Alice paused, as if this were an entirely new facet to the case. "I don't know about that."

"Are your mother and father getting a divorce?"

"Heavens no! My mother's a Catholic. She almost became a nun."

"Your father knows you're getting married?"

"I wrote him about it."

"Have you had an answer?"

"Not recently."

"How come you didn't marry Bill Whipple? You seemed to like him well enough."

Alice turned Joe a startled look. "What do you mean?"

"You went out to Halfway House with him."

"How do you know about that?" asked Alice breathlessly. "Does Marsh know?"

"No." Joe showed her the photograph. Alice stared at the picture as if it held the secret to her life. "That was so long ago... I felt so young then."

"You're young now."

Alice gave a wistful grimace. "I told you I'm not respectable."

"You're probably as respectable as most people. It seems to me you're just reacting to an overdose of respectability."

Alice heaved a sigh. "Probably so."

"Was this the first time you went out with Bill?"

Alice gave her head a quick shake. "The second time." She laughed. "He asked me to marry him... Poor Bill."

"What did you say?"

"No. Bill didn't really love me. He was mad about Starr. She wouldn't look at him. He asked me out to spite her. And Marsh and all the Short-ridges. That's why he wanted to marry me — from spite."

"Don't talk yourself down."

"It's true enough. And as far as I was concerned — well, I wasn't very happy. I really didn't want to be engaged to Marsh. I don't have very much will power... Not very much decency, I suppose."

"Did your mother know about you and Bill?"

Alice winced. "She detested Bill. She thought he was vulgar and heathen."

"Seems to me that your mother runs things around here."

"Well, not altogether. As far as Bill was concerned, I didn't want to marry him. I was being defiant toward my mother and Marsh. Bill was defying Starr." Alice laughed — a forlorn sound. "Starr couldn't care less what Bill or I did."

Joe rubbed his chin. "Forget I'm sheriff. Pretend I'm an old friend."

"That's not hard." Alice gave Joe a smile that made his head swim.

"You're Catholic like your mother?"

"I've never had much choice. I guess — yes."

"You don't believe in divorce, things like that?"

"I — guess not."

"Well, you better ditch Marsh now, before the knot is tied. Otherwise you're stuck with him."

Alice smiled wanly. "If I did, who'd support us? Myself and Mother and now there's a little baby. None of us knows how to earn a living. It would kill Mother to give up the house."

"Your father undoubtedly will furnish child support."

Alice made a sudden gesture of fatigue. "I'm so sick of the entire business! I can understand how people sometimes want to kill themselves."

"Here, here," said Joe. "Things aren't that bad. Heavens, for two cents I'd marry you myself. Except I've got a daughter not much younger than you. It would look silly. Howard Griselda would take me to task in an editorial."

Alice laughed, and looked so charming that for a wild instant Joe thought that he might propose in earnest. Alice asked, rather archly, "Even after you know how wicked I've been?"

"We'd both be taking our chances."

"You don't know how bad I really am."

"How bad is that?" asked Joe. "Does it extend to hitting Ken and Bill and Mrs. Wagner with a hammer?"

"Oh no. I could never hurt anyone. Physically..." Her voice drifted away. Then she said, "You can come to my wedding."

"Not even second best," said Joe. "Oh well, that's neither here nor there. I probably couldn't stand your mother. I sure as hell wouldn't support her."

Alice nodded as if this were precisely the point she had been trying to make. "Right now I feel a hundred years old. All I can think about is peace and quiet."

"No more wild oats?"

"No. I've finished."

"And who was the most recent boy friend? I'm asking now officially."

"It was nothing serious. Please don't ask me his name. Because I won't tell you."

Joe reflected. "Let me look at your passport. If you got back after Sally Wagner died, I suppose it doesn't make any great difference."

Alice wordlessly left the room, returned a moment later with her passport. Joe checked the stamp at the port of entry: *San Francisco, August 1.* "How come your mother hasn't seen this date?"

"She never looked. She disapproved of the European trip — pretended that it never existed."

"I'll bet you a dollar she knows everything that's in that passport."

Alice shrugged listlessly. "I don't care. I'm just tired of everything. Worry, poverty, being dutiful."

"Don't say I never advised you," said Joe.

2

Joe went out to his car, head buzzing with thoughts. Impossible to suspect Alice of homicide. She was too sad, too beautiful, too sweet-natured. What did she have to gain? Furthermore, she was six thousand miles away at the time of the murders.

Suppose, thought Joe, just suppose, that Starr Shortridge was really mad about Bill Whipple, that she had been dissembling her love all these years. Suppose then that she heard about the Christmas party at Halfway House — was it conceivable that the news would have driven her into a state of insane rage?

A theory even less convincing than most of his others. But for want of anything better Joe drove his car up the Shortridge driveway, parked, rang the doorbell. To his relief Starr herself answered the ring; Joe was not up to facing Miriam Shortridge's cool stare.

"Hello, Sheriff," said Starr. She came out on the terrace.

"Hello, Miss Shortridge," said Joe. "Tell me, did you commit three murders out of unrequited love for Bill Whipple?"

"No."

"I didn't expect you had. Do you know who did?"

"Not really."

"Naturally you know Alice is home from Europe."

Starr nodded. "Marsh has had her here to dinner — twice. She's a patient girl. I wouldn't marry Marsh for all the money in the world."

Marsh drove up in his white Ford hardtop, alighted, paused to look at Joe. Then, nodding curtly, he came forward. "What's new, Sheriff?"

"I've just been talking to Miss Benjamin and your sister, hoping for some fresh ideas."

"It's time fresh ideas were coming from somewhere."

"I keep learning things," said Joe. "I have the curious feeling that something obvious is lurking just out of sight; that if I turned my head quick I'd see it…I take it you haven't thought of anything which might have a bearing on the case?"

"Not a thing."

"I guess you're getting pretty excited, wedding so close and all."

Marsh opened his mouth, then closed it. If he said yes, he subscribed to Joe's arch whimsy. If he said no, he became a churl. "It's something everyone has to bear up under," he said stiffly.

"Out of curiosity, are you turning Catholic?"

Again Marsh struggled to find words. Starr looked off up Spanish Hill, face grave and impassive.

"I was brought up to Episcopalian doctrine," said Marsh. "Alice's church asked me to take instruction and I had no profound objection; essentially the teachings are similar."

"The Catholics use more incense," said Starr.

Marsh deigned no reply.

"Where does the wedding take place?" asked Joe. "I might even come."

"It's to be a private affair," said Marsh. "It will take place here at the house."

"Oh? Not in the Catholic church? I thought that was the accepted thing."

"We've decided upon a civil ceremony," said Marsh tersely.

Starr amplified the remark. "Marsh was married once before, to a musician. And divorced, of course. It won't be bigamy."

"What's your opinion," asked Joe, "on divorce and contraception and affairs like that?"

"I hold conservative views," said Marsh. "I really don't care to discuss the subject."

"Sorry," said Joe. "I understand that you and Bill Whipple had a big fight a week or so before his death."

Marsh glared at Starr, who returned an expression of limpid innocence. Marsh looked away, mouth turned savagely down at the corners. "It wasn't a week before," he muttered. "It was two days before. He'd been bothering Starr. He thought to attack her through me and made some vile accusations."

"Against whom?"

"That's quite irrelevant."

"In a murder case nothing is irrelevant."

Marsh paid no heed. "There was no 'big fight', as you put it. I merely told him off. He'd always had a very strange attitude toward Starr and myself, some sort of emotional instability: ambivalence, I think it's called."

"That's no reason to kill him."

Marsh stuttered with indignation. "Are you suggesting that I killed him?"

"Somebody did."

Marsh turned on his heel, strode into the house. Joe gave a rueful shake of his head and departed.

3

Back at headquarters, Joe immured himself in his office and tried to think.

If the motive for the killings derived from Mrs. Bazzarini's money, then Caspar Hubman and/or Laura Hubman were the prime suspects.

If the murders stemmed from the Christmas party at Halfway House, then the people most obviously, if remotely, motivated included Marsh, Alice's parents and Helen Ferguson's parents. The Fergusons, not resident on Madrone Way, could be dismissed. Grace Benjamin had been too pregnant to get into Ken's uniform, let alone wheel Bill Whipple in a wheelbarrow, or climb the fence intervening between her house and Sally Wagner's. Guy Benjamin was in India.

Joe sat up in his chair. He reached for his telephone, called the Benjamin house.

Mrs. Benjamin responded. In the background could be heard the whimpering of the baby.

"Sheriff Joe Bain here, Mrs. Benjamin. Whom does your husband work for?"

"An engineering company which is building a dam in India."

"Which company?"

"The Amonette Construction Company, 29 King James Parade, Darjeeling, India."

"Where is the home office of the company?"

"In San Francisco."

"Thank you, Mrs. Benjamin."

Joe telephoned the Amonette Construction Company in San Francisco and was connected to the personnel department. "This is Joe Bain, Sheriff of San Rodrigo County. I want some information regarding one of your employees."

"Very sorry, sir. We don't give out information regarding our people over the telephone."

"All I want is his address."

"Sorry, sir. You can write him in care of this office."

"Confound it, I'm Sheriff of San Rodrigo County, a law-enforcement officer. Call me back if you don't believe me."

"It's firm company policy, sir. I can't do anything about it. If you'll bring your credentials to the office or submit your question by registered mail on official stationery, we'll help you as much as we can."

Joe hung up, sat seething on the edge of his chair. A minute passed. He jumped to his feet, spoke briefly to Ace Wardell and Miss Curdy, then, cursing and muttering, started north for San Francisco.

4

The headquarters of the Amonette Construction Company occupied the eleventh floor of the Golden State Building on Montgomery Street. Joe walked along a corridor separated by glass panels from an enormous drafting room, entered through a door bearing the inscription PERSONNEL DEPARTMENT. A brisk young man in a white shirt and bow tie came to the counter. "Yes, sir?"

Joe opened his wallet, displayed his badge. "I want to talk with the head of the department."

"Mr. Trask, sir. Just a minute."

Joe was ushered into an office twice as large as his own, decorated by photographs of jobs and crews. Trask rose to his feet, a man a foot taller than Joe with a great gaunt face, the mildest of brown eyes, a few sparse strands of hair.

Joe once more displayed his badge, which Trask inspected with amiable interest. "And what's your problem?"

"I want some information in regard to one of your engineers, Mr. Guy Benjamin. I want proof or at least high-level assurance that he is in India and has been there since the first of the year."

Trask leaned back in his chair, folded his hands on his chest, shook his big head. "I can't help you."

"Eh? How come?"

"Guy Benjamin's been here at the home office since spring."

"What!" cried Joe. "Here in San Francisco?"

"Go into the third office down the hall," said Trask. "Maybe Benjamin can prove he's in India. I can't."

Joe ran his fingers through his hair. "The least I can do is ask him."

The door to the third office down the hall carried the information CHIEF EXPEDITER.

Joe entered. The air reeked with cigarette smoke. Three desks were crowded into the room; at each a man in shirtsleeves sat talking earnestly into a telephone. None of the men was Guy Benjamin, none of them did more than glance up.

Joe crossed the room, looked into the inner office. Here sat Guy

Benjamin, tapping a calculator and making check marks on a list. He looked up. "Yes, sir?"

Joe studied him a moment before speaking: the redoubtable Grace Benjamin's husband. Joe wondered why. Guy Benjamin was a slender man with an easy indolent face, well-brushed bronze hair, a neat bronze mustache. In some indefinable way he looked old-fashioned, like an early photograph of John Gilbert. It was apparent, thought Joe, that Alice had inherited both her charm and her flexibility — 'weakness' was much too strong a word — from her father. Grace Benjamin was of a different mettle.

"I'm Joe Bain, Sheriff of San Rodrigo County." Joe displayed his badge.

Guy Benjamin nodded glumly. He pointed to a chair. "Sit down, Sheriff."

Joe drew the chair forward. "I'm surprised to find you here. I understood you to be in India."

Guy Benjamin made a small gesture, implying that this was the impression he wanted to give. "I had the chance to transfer home; I took it. Much more comfortable here. Although Darjeeling isn't really all that bad."

"Have you been in communication with Pleasant Grove?" Joe asked delicately.

"I'm afraid not," said Guy Benjamin with a faint smile.

"You know what's been going on along Madrone Way?"

"I can't say as I do."

"When was your last visit to Pleasant Grove?"

"The holiday season of last year. I doubt if I'll be going back. My wife and I have come to an understanding. She won't divorce me, I can't divorce her. So — she lives her life; I live mine. What's going on that's so all-fired exciting?"

"I'll come to that in a minute or two," said Joe. "You know your daughter is getting married."

Guy Benjamin nodded, offered Joe a cigarette. Joe refused. Guy Benjamin struck a match, lit up. He said, "I wouldn't pick Marsh Shortridge myself but after all I don't have to live with him."

"You're not going to the wedding?"

Guy Benjamin shook his head. "I'd have to be civil to Grace; I might slip. Why risk it?"

"Alice doesn't know you're here?"

"No. She'd tell her mother, which isn't in my scheme of things. I'm not heartless, Sheriff, just gutless. You don't know Grace. That woman is the original irresistible force. She put me through the wringer; I gave her the house as a financial settlement, which she found satisfactory. I've been making Alice an allowance of a hundred and fifty a month, which naturally I'm glad to do. Aside from that I'm on my own."

"What of the baby?" asked Joe. "Aren't you interested in taking care of your child?"

"What baby?" asked Guy. "You don't mean Alice. She's Marsh's baby now."

"I mean young Beatrice, whom Grace gave birth to last month."

Guy Benjamin sat bolt upright in his chair, mustache bristling. "Grace has a baby?"

"I'll vouch for it myself."

"My, my, my," murmured Guy Benjamin, slumping back into the chair and pulling at his mustache. "This is indeed a surprise...I won't go into any details, but whoever the father is, include me out."

Joe frowned in perplexity. "You mean that when you were home last winter you didn't sleep with her?"

"Those were the details I wasn't going into. I did not. Well, well, well. This is utterly fantastic. Grace. Her religion. Her qualms. Her scruples. Her religion. Her ethics. Her religion..."

Joe scratched his head. "Who in the world is the father?"

"If you ask me," said Guy Benjamin, "it's an immaculate conception. Will you be so kind as to tell me what in tarnation you're here for?"

"Do you know Ken Mooney?"

"No."

"How about Bill Whipple?"

"I know young Bill. Girl-chaser from up the street."

"And Sally Wagner?"

"Sally Wagner, of course."

"Well, they're all dead — murdered." Joe described the crimes.

Guy Benjamin laughed weakly. He stubbed out his cigarette, leaned back in his chair. "I don't have any alibi. The theory of my killing these people is so far-fetched I can't even worry about it."

"This is the case with all my suspects," said Joe. "If you could definitely clear yourself you'd be helping me locate the real killer."

"I'm dreadfully sorry, Sheriff. I can't prove where I was two days ago, much less a month."

Joe sat back, glumly considering Guy Benjamin, whose presence in San Francisco he had hoped would be a break in the case.

"Incidentally," inquired Guy Benjamin, "are you informing Grace of my whereabouts?"

"If I make inquiries about the baby —"

Guy Benjamin winced. "That'll take guts."

"— I'll have to bring you into it."

Guy Benjamin threw up his hands. "I might as well go to the wedding. I am fond of Alice." He squinted off through the window, where the afternoon sunlight slanted across the building opposite. "When I think back, oh Lord it seems so long ago, what a young fool I was…"

"That's how people go mad," said Joe. "Well, it's getting late. I don't know whether you've helped matters or not."

"If I were guilty, I'd be glad to confess," said Guy Benjamin politely. "Just to save you further trouble."

Joe rose to his feet. "Why can't everyone be so considerate?" He brought out his notebook. "I'll want your address and telephone number. Please call me before you make any moves, or out of sheer hysteria I might have you arrested."

5

Joe returned south down Highway 101 to San Jose, then swung off at a slant to Aurora, where he telephoned Luna. "Have you had dinner yet?"

"No," said Luna. "I've been so terribly busy, I haven't had time even to think of eating."

"If I brought over two large steaks, a loaf of French bread and a six-pack, do you think we could manage?"

"I'll start some onions frying."

After dinner Joe helped Luna shift the concrete pans into a possibly more effective configuration. Then they sat in the lawn swing discussing the murders. "I have a feeling I'm right on top of the case," said Joe. "But why? why? why? Why kill Ken Mooney? Why kill Bill Whipple? Why kill Sally Wagner? Grace Benjamin couldn't hope to conceal her baby. If Laura or Caspar Hubman wanted to protect their inheritance they wouldn't kill Ken on his route, they'd do something more subtle. Marsh Shortridge is too much of a poltroon to slaughter anybody. Starr doesn't give a damn. Alice Benjamin was in Europe. Guy Benjamin..." Joe shook his head. "I'm running around in circles."

"When is the wedding?"

"In about a week."

"Are you going to ask Mrs. Benjamin about the father of the baby?"

"Hell, no. She'd just say it's none of my business. And I'd say, 'Mrs. Benjamin, in a murder case, everything is my business'. Then she'd change the subject. I can't put her in jail for refusing to state who she was sleeping with."

Luna shook her head dubiously. "Even I find this very confusing."

CHAPTER XIII

1

THE WEEK WENT BY. On the morning of September 20 three youths, sixteen, seventeen and eighteen years old, robbed a bank in San Jose and fled into San Rodrigo County. Joe, deploying his entire crew, herded the bandits toward a Highway Patrol road-block. They approached at ninety miles an hour, tried to make a screeching turn, spun out of control into a ditch, rolled out again and down the road, amid a hellish crunching din. There were no survivors.

During the afternoon the Shortridge-Benjamin wedding rehearsal took place; afterwards the Benjamins were guests at the Shortridge house for dinner.

Joe, in a travail of dissatisfaction, paced the living room floor until his mother, unable to watch TV, became disgusted and went to bed.

"Don't ever get elected sheriff," Joe told Miranda. "It's the shortest route to gray hairs... How is it that old Cucchinello never had these problems? He died a happy man."

Miranda tried to soothe him. "Something will turn up."

"That's not how I want it!" Joe exclaimed. "I'm supposed to be in charge; I'm supposed to be able to figure things out. Can Howard Griselda be right? Am I a meathead? I'm swaying over toward that opinion."

"Now, Daddy, remember what you've always told me. If you don't have faith in yourself, nobody else will either."

"True. I also know what a miserable fiasco these murders have been."

"Let's think together," suggested Miranda. "First of all, we know the murders weren't suicide."

"Right," said Joe. "We can also eliminate death through the onslaught of enraged canaries."

"Now you're being sarcastic." Miranda sniffed. "I was just trying to help."

"I know, I know." Joe paced up and down. "Go snatch open a can of beer. For me, not you. It helps to lubricate my thinking processes."

Three cans of beer lubricated Joe's thinking processes to such an extent that he went to bed.

Next morning at his office he continued pondering. Sheer logic ought to solve these crimes. "Sally Wagner did it merely by looking at a wheelbarrow," Joe told himself, "and she didn't know as much as I know. I guess I don't have a flexible mind. I should be speculating more freely instead of trying to prove things. For instance, what if someone has been living in the Mortimer house all this time? What if Marsh never got divorced? Who is the father to Grace Benjamin's child? Marsh? Ken? Bill? Caspar Hubman?"

Joe jerked upright as if Miss Curdy had dropped an ice cube down his neck.

"Can it be? Could it happen?" He looked at his watch. Nine forty-five, with the wedding in fifteen minutes. "If I'm wrong I might as well pack my clothes and emigrate."

2

Madrone Way was dense with parked cars; Joe pulled up into the Shortridge driveway as far as he could go.

The old house wore a festive air. Bouquets of red and white carnations decorated the balustrade; from within came the sound of a string quartet.

Joe ran up the steps, pushed his way into the great living room. The wedding had not yet started. At the end of the room an altar and a pulpit had been set up. White candles burned in bronze candelabra. Guests were everywhere: important folk from the whole of San Rodrigo County. By the altar stood Sam Shortridge in formal morning attire, Milo Gentry, Howard Griselda, Mr. and Mrs. Wilfred Mortimer, Laura Hubman, Grace Benjamin, and Porter Barrett, owner of Rancho La Zuñada in the Indian Hills.

Joe approached the group, tapped Sam Shortridge's arm, signaled him aside. "I'm sorry to barge in just at this time, Mr. Shortridge…"

"Not at all, Sheriff," said Sam Shortridge jovially. "Glad you could make it. We're just about ready to throw open the chute."

"This is a very awkward situation," said Joe in a worried voice. "Maybe the wedding had better be postponed."

Sam Shortridge's face became loose in wonder. "What did you say? Postpone the wedding?"

Joe put on his most affable smile. "Now is a peculiar time to be investigating a murder, but ten minutes ago I finally got things straight. Or so I hope."

Miriam Shortridge, effulgent in pink, approached. "What is the trouble, Sam?"

Sam Shortridge said in a puzzled voice, "The Sheriff wants to postpone the wedding."

"That's simply ridiculous!" exclaimed Miriam Shortridge. "How in the world can he even think of such a thing?"

"What's all this?" demanded Grace Benjamin, and once again Sam Shortridge explained Joe's request. Grace Benjamin said to Joe: "You must be insane."

Joe opened his mouth but Howard Griselda spoke first. "Sheriff Bain has a regrettable flair for spectacle and melodrama."

"Excuse me for disagreeing, Mr. Griselda," said Joe. "I could easily let the marriage proceed, but there might be a lot of consternation afterwards. Then everyone would come at me and say, 'Sheriff Bain, you callous rumdum, why didn't you halt the ceremony?'"

Sam Shortridge, suddenly haggard and harried, said, "Just what do you have in mind?"

Joe rubbed his chin irresolutely. He looked around the room. To the side, Guy Benjamin, bland and self-possessed, chatted with Caspar Hubman. Starr, wearing a bright green frock, sat grimly on a couch with young Orlando Bennett, son of Basil Bennett, Aurora's most distinguished attorney.

Joe said slowly, "The easiest thing might be for you just to announce that the wedding has been postponed."

Grace Benjamin made a bleating sound. "I won't have it. I think it's disgraceful. Couldn't all this wait till after the ceremony?"

"I'm sorry, Mrs. Benjamin. It's a miserable situation. But don't forget, three people have been killed, which is even more miserable." He met Howard Griselda's sardonic glance, turned to Sam Shortridge. "I want to ask a few questions. I can either do it in private or out in front of everybody, which will be more embarrassing but quicker."

"Embarrassing for whom?" inquired Miriam Shortridge.

Sam Shortridge made an impatient gesture. "Get on with it, get it over with. It'll be public property in any event."

"Please call in Marsh and Alice."

Miriam Shortridge started to protest, but Sam cut her short. "Do as the Sheriff requests. He's not fooling."

"I hope I'm not," muttered Joe. Alice, in her wedding gown, Marsh in formal morning clothes, along with Charles Beasley, his best man, wonderingly entered the room. Sam Shortridge gave them a peremptory signal. "Over here. Sheriff Bain is halting the marriage."

Marsh began to swell with outrage. Sam Shortridge in a brittle voice said, "First let's hear what he has to tell us."

Joe hesitated. "You're sure you don't want this in private? There's going to be some ticklish subjects raised."

"Get on with it," rasped Sam Shortridge.

Joe shrugged. "Maybe it's the best way. Mr. Benjamin, will you please step over here?"

Guy Benjamin approached.

"Mr. Benjamin, are you the father of Beatrice Benjamin?"

"No," said Guy Benjamin pleasantly. "I am not. Very definitely."

Miriam Shortridge gasped and made a hissing noise between her teeth.

"Is this true, Mrs. Benjamin?" asked Joe.

Grace Benjamin went geranium red. "What an outrageous thing to ask!"

"Well, now that I've asked it, what's the answer?"

"I refuse to discuss the subject."

"Can we see the baby's birth certificate?"

"You can see nothing."

"In which hospital was the baby born? Who was the doctor who attended you?"

"That is none of your affair."

"Come now, Mrs. Benjamin. This is a perfectly innocent question. Nobody is going to crucify you for an indiscretion; just tell us where the baby was born, and the name of the doctor."

"I refuse to discuss my personal affairs in public."

"Will you tell me in private?"

"I'll tell you nothing whatever. It's none of your business."

"Your last chance to answer, Mrs. Benjamin. Where was the baby born? Who was the doctor?"

Howard Griselda said impatiently, "There's no point in not supplying the information, Mrs. Benjamin."

"No. I won't. I won't deign to answer."

Joe turned to Starr, who sat frozen-faced on the couch, then looked at Marsh and Alice. "Seven or eight years ago you three demolished a tree-house built by Bill Whipple. True?"

"True," said Marsh, in a nervous and high-pitched voice.

"What happened to the tools?" He looked from face to face.

Alice said haltingly, "I took them. I gave them to my father."

Guy Benjamin nodded. "Yes, I remember. Quite distinctly. A hammer and a saw."

"That hammer killed three people." Joe turned to Alice. "Do you know where Beatrice Benjamin was born?"

Alice glanced at her mother. Joe stepped forward. "Just answer my question."

Alice said in a quavering voice, "I'm not sure…"

"Do you or do you not know?"

"Yes, I do."

Grace Benjamin said, "He has no right to inquire into my private business. Don't tell him a thing."

Alice looked pleadingly at Joe. "I don't want to answer."

"I'm sorry, Miss Benjamin, but it's all got to come out. All. Everything. You arrived home from Europe August first. Correct?"

"What?" cried Marsh.

Alice heaved a deep shuddering sigh. "Yes."

"Did you try to telephone Bill Whipple, to tell him that you were pregnant with his child, only to find that he was dead?"

"Alice!" blared Grace Benjamin. "Don't you dare say a word!"

"Yes!" cried Alice. "I'm sick of the whole thing! I'm glad to tell the truth! I did! I did."

Marsh gave a croak of dismay. Sam Shortridge, dumfounded, stood looking from face to face. Guy Benjamin examined his fingernails. Starr Shortridge laughed: a merry rollicking laugh.

"Ken Mooney was killed on a very hot day," said Joe. "The Taylor kids had a lemonade stand going. Ken bought a glass of lemonade on credit. He collected some money on a C.O.D. package from Marsh, but he never paid the Taylor boys. Ken never left Madrone Way. He had a registered letter for Mrs. Benjamin, which was never delivered. Superficially it would seem that somewhere along in here Ken was killed. The murderer should therefore be a Shortridge, a Taylor or a Benjamin, who thereupon got into Ken's uniform and delivered the rest of the mail.

"It wasn't a Taylor. Mrs. Benjamin was ostensibly pregnant. She really wasn't. She got herself into the situation by the most ridiculous blunder imaginable. It's no wonder that she hated Sally Wagner. It's so tragic it's funny. Sally Wagner found her buying pregnancy capsules or vitamins or some such stuff, and Grace Benjamin was so rattled that she admitted to being pregnant. It seemed the only way out at the time, and oh what trouble it caused! Actually Mrs. Benjamin was buying pills for Alice.

"Mrs. Benjamin's religion wouldn't allow an abortion. She anticipated Alice having a quiet birth somewhere, then putting the baby out for adoption and going along with the marriage as planned. Grace Benjamin desperately needs this marriage. She's broke. If Marsh doesn't marry Alice and make her an allowance she'll have to go to work. But alas: Sally Wagner surprised her. All Grace Benjamin could think to say was that yes, she was pregnant. It was the worst misfortune of her life. Because after that she had to act out being pregnant. It also meant she had to keep the baby.

"One hot day—June eighteenth, to be precise—Ken Mooney comes along with a registered letter. Now this is my guess. I suspect he rang the bell, got no answer and decided that Mrs. Benjamin was in the back yard. He pushed open the gate, walked around the house — and there, lo and behold! was Grace Benjamin fixing a trellis or hammering stakes for her chrysanthemums, maybe in a sun-suit? Anyway, without her padding. She was straight as a pencil! Ken probably stood stock-still and said, 'Why, Mrs. Benjamin! I thought you were pregnant!' Or maybe he didn't say a word, but just looked in amazement.

"Mrs. Benjamin sees her world crumbling. Ken's next stop is Sally Wagner's. The whole story is sure to come out. Grace can almost hear Sally Wagner laughing. Unluckily for Ken, there at hand is the hammer Alice brought down from the hill. She clouts Ken in a sudden terrible fury. The rest we know. What about it, Mrs. Benjamin?"

The room was quiet.

Howard Griselda cleared his throat. "Mrs. Benjamin, is the allegation true or false?"

Grace Benjamin said, "False, of course! There's no evidence whatever for all this! It's slander, defamation."

"It certainly is," said Joe, "provided that it's not true. There's one bit of evidence: the *Life* magazine. When you clouted Ken you took the magazine he had just brought you, shoved it under his head. Afterwards when you thought about it, you tore your name from the cover. After the body was found you got thinking that inevitably the police would check on the *Life*. You bought a *Life* from the drug store, soaked away an old label, pasted it on the cover. You probably didn't think that this made one too many *Lifes*. I'll pick up that *Life* and use it in court."

Alice was drooping, sagging, staring at Joe with glazed eyes. Marsh, suddenly ridiculous in his finery, had gone limp.

Joe went on. "Alice doesn't particularly want to marry Marsh. She doesn't want to marry anybody. She was probably half in love with Bill Whipple; at least he appealed to the woman in her. She might have called him in the spring, when she first learned she was pregnant."

"He said no!" cried Alice. "He didn't want to get married!"

"I'd say he showed poor taste," stated Joe gallantly. "Well, be that as it may, for some mysterious reason, he changed his mind."

Starr spoke in a clear voice. "The reason is not all that mysterious. He was furious with me, and thought he saw a way to get even."

"Maybe so. Well, he went out to Halfway House for a photograph he remembered sticking on the wall, then he went to see Mrs. Benjamin, maybe to ask Alice's address, maybe to acquaint her with the way things were going to be. I imagine the conversation went something like this. Bill says, 'Mrs. Benjamin, Alice and I are getting married. I'm going to make her an honest woman and give our child a wonderful home'. 'What child? What are you talking about?' asks Grace Benjamin, already reaching for the hammer. 'I mean the baby I bred out at Halfway House last Christmas. See this picture?' 'But Alice is engaged to wealthy young Marsh Shortridge,' says Grace Benjamin. 'Can you support us in the same style that Marsh Shortridge can?' 'No, I can't. Furthermore I don't intend to try. So give me her address, otherwise I'm on my way to see Marsh Shortridge.' 'Well, okay, if that's the way you want it. Hand me my pencil, I dropped it on the floor.' As Bill reaches for the pencil: *whack*! with the hammer.

"The wheelbarrow is handy. Late at night Grace Benjamin trundles Bill Whipple up the street and dumps him behind Mrs. Bazzarini's shed."

Howard Griselda once more looked toward Grace Benjamin. "Is this true, Mrs. Benjamin?"

"There's not a jot of evidence," said Grace Benjamin. "Not a jot or tittle."

"There's a great deal of evidence," said Joe. "Once we realize your pregnancy was a fake, there's evidence everywhere. The wheelbarrow, for instance. It started Sally Wagner thinking. I couldn't figure out what she saw even though you told us a dozen times to be careful of your new lawn. The murderer very fastidiously had circled the new lawn, about a hundred feet out of his way, both coming and going. The murderer was lawn-conscious, even while wheeling a corpse. Strange! Sally Wagner saw this right away. But thinking you seven months pregnant, it all seemed impossible. But you saw her and you knew what she was thinking. You knew she wouldn't let the matter rest. Maybe she was more definite, maybe she made her suspicions clear in some unmistakable manner. There I can't even imagine what happened. But you knew that Sally Wagner was about to break things wide open. How to get at her? She kept her doors locked. Since she suspected you, sure as thunder she wouldn't let you into the house. This is how you solved the problem, or so I imagine. It probably came to you as you stood in your upstairs window watching Sally Wagner burn trash in her incinerator. I'll insert the information that we haven't been able to locate the person to whom Sally Wagner was talking when she was killed. Why not? Because it was you. Sally Wagner's telephone rings; she rushes into the house, not bothering to lock the back door. Then you say something like this, in a disguised voice, 'Mrs. Sally Wagner? Long Distance call from Washington D.C. Please hold the line.' Then it's quick over the fence by the step-ladder and into the house. Sally Wagner sits with her ear glued to the telephone. *Whack!* with the hammer. And you're off to the shower at Mrs. Taylor's house. But after you hung up the telephone you forgot the hammer. Not a bad mistake, you thought. Nobody will recognize that old thing.

"It just so happened that the hammer figured in another little drama eight years or so previously. Lots of people remember the hammer." Joe sighed. "There it is, Mrs. Benjamin. That's the story. You don't have to say a word until you've seen a lawyer."

Grace Benjamin seemed neither perturbed nor unduly distressed. She stood thinking, mouth moving in and out as if she were chewing thread. Howard Griselda stared in fascination. Guy Benjamin turned away to study a bouquet of red and white carnations. Alice suddenly screamed. She screamed again and again, fists clenched in the air beside her shoulders. Then she ran from the room, down the steps, down the driveway and off along Madrone Way, her wedding gown fluttering. Marsh hesitated a grudging instant, then muttered something under his breath and ran after her.

Grace Benjamin paid no heed. She asked Joe, "Am I under arrest?"

"Yes, Mrs. Benjamin."

"There is no evidence against me."

"The jury can decide that."

3

Searching the Benjamin house, Joe and Rex Kelly found that copy of *Life* dated June 21, purportedly delivered by Ken Mooney on the last day of his existence.

Joe held the label to the light. "Look at that smear. It's airplane cement, something of the sort. We've got her cold."

Chapter XIV

1

At the trial Grace Benjamin's attorney argued that the entire case of the prosecution was circumstantial, indirect and hypothetical; that no single direct link connected Mrs. Benjamin with the murders. He dismissed the *Life* magazine, the hammer, the fictitious pregnancy as inconsequential.

The judge instructed the jury that circumstantial evidence was as good as any, that they were not required to invent improbable or fantastic alternate hypotheses. The jury found the defendant guilty and made no recommendations for mercy. Mrs. Benjamin heard the verdict in stony silence, and was sentenced to life imprisonment.

2

Guy Benjamin requested and secured a transfer back to India. Alice and the baby went with him. Marsh Shortridge became more terse, more clenched, more bitter than ever. Starr suddenly decided to travel and would not be denied. She wandered to London, took a job as a receptionist and presently married a marine architect.

On Madrone Way the three houses in which had lived the Benjamins, the Whipples and Sally Wagner were put on the market and presently sold. Three new families moved to Madrone Way and life went on as before.

3

In San Francisco newspapers appeared an advertisement:

⚞ HALFWAY HOUSE ⚟

The historic old stagecoach stop on
the road between Monterey and Vallejo
is now an old-fashioned country hotel.
Home-cooked meals. No TV, no juke-box.

— MARIAN BAIN, MANAGER —

Contreras Road, seven miles south of Jordan
San Rodrigo County

Miranda decided that she absolutely needed a car. Joe jestingly told her to fire up the 1926 Marmon roadster in the barn to the back of Halfway House. To Joe's dismay and Marian Bain's horror she accepted with enthusiasm. Five young bucks appeared with tools; the Marmon was overhauled, rechromed, repainted, refurbished, and presently became the rage of Pleasant Grove High School.

Miranda was thought lucky to have such a wonderful father.

4

Luna was called to another destination.

"Arthemisia?" Joe asked.

"No, not yet," replied Luna. "I'm needed once again in Texas. But after that, who knows where?"

"Drop me a postcard from wherever you are," said Joe.

"I'll remember… I'm so sorry to leave."

"I'm sorry to have you leave. Things are going to be much too sedate. I'll never want to drive out Hankinson Road any more. I love this little house out here under the trees. Especially at sunset when the wind blows up out of the valley."

"Now don't. You'll have me crying in a minute. I've got to say goodbye."

"Goodbye, Luna."

"Goodbye, Joe."

JACK VANCE was born in 1916 to a well-off California family that, as his childhood ended, fell upon hard times. As a young man he worked at a series of unsatisfying jobs before studying mining engineering, physics, journalism and English at the University of California Berkeley. Leaving school as America was going to war, he found a place as an ordinary seaman in the merchant marine. Later he worked as a rigger, surveyor, ceramicist, and carpenter before his steady production of sf, mystery novels, and short stories established him as a full-time writer.

His output over more than sixty years was prodigious and won him three Hugo Awards, a Nebula Award, a World Fantasy Award for lifetime achievement, as well as an Edgar from the Mystery Writers of America. The Science Fiction and Fantasy Writers of America named him a grandmaster and he was inducted into the Science Fiction Hall of Fame.

His works crossed genre boundaries, from dark fantasies (including the highly influential *Dying Earth* cycle of novels) to interstellar space operas, from heroic fantasy (the *Lyonesse* trilogy) to murder mysteries featuring a sheriff (the Joe Bain novels) in a rural California county. A Vance story often centered on a competent male protagonist thrust into a dangerous, evolving situation on a planet where adventure was his daily fare, or featured a young person setting out on a perilous odyssey over difficult terrain populated by entrenched, scheming enemies.

Late in his life, a world-spanning assemblage of Vance aficionados came together to return his works to their original form, restoring material cut by editors whose chief preoccupation was the page count of a pulp magazine. The result was the complete and authoritative *Vance Integral Edition* in 44 hardcover volumes. Spatterlight Press is now publishing the VIE texts as ebooks, and as print-on-demand paperbacks.

Colophon

This book was printed using Adobe Arno Pro as the primary text font, with NeutraFace used on the cover.

This title was created from the digital archive of the Vance Integral Edition, a series of 44 books produced under the aegis of the author by a worldwide group of his readers. The VIE project gratefully acknowledges the editorial guidance of Norma Vance, as well as the cooperation of the Department of Special Collections at Boston University, whose John Holbrook Vance collection has been an important source of textual evidence.

Special thanks to R.C. Lacovara, Patrick Dusoulier, Koen Vyverman, Paul Rhoads, Chuck King, Gregory Hansen, Suan Yong, and Josh Geller for their invaluable assistance preparing final versions of the source files.

Digitize: Mark Adams, Mike Dennison, Billy Webb, Dave Worden; Format: John A. Schwab; Diff: David A. Kennedy, Hans van der Veeke; Tech Proof: Hans van der Veeke; Text Integrity: Paul Rhoads, Steve Sherman, Tim Stretton; Implement: Derek W. Benson, Hans van der Veeke; Security: Paul Rhoads; Compose: Andreas Irle; Comp Review: Marcel van Genderen, Brian Gharst, Charles King, Bob Luckin; Update Verify: Rob Friefeld, Marcel van Genderen, Bob Luckin, Paul Rhoads, Robin L. Rouch; RTF-Diff: Mark Bradford, Errico Rescigno; Textport: Patrick Dusoulier; Proofread: Erik Arendse, Michel Bazin, Angus Campbell-Cann, Christian J. Corley, Patrick Dusoulier, Marcel van Genderen, Yannick Gour, Erec Grim, Jasper Groen, Jurriaan Kalkman, Till Noever, Willem Timmer, Hans van der Veeke, Dirk Jan Verlinde

Artwork (maps based on original drawings by Jack and Norma Vance):

Paul Rhoads, Christopher Wood

Book Composition and Typesetting: Joel Anderson

Art Direction and Cover Design: Howard Kistler

Proofing: Christian J. Corley, Steve Sherman

Jacket Blurb: John Vance

Management: John Vance, Koen Vyverman